Praise for
Carlton Mellick III

"Easily the craziest, weirdest, strangest, funniest, most obscene writer in America."
—*GOTHIC MAGAZINE*

"Carlton Mellick III has the craziest book titles... and the kinkiest fans!"
—CHRISTOPHER MOORE, author of *The Stupidest Angel*

"If you haven't read Mellick you're not nearly perverse enough for the twenty first century."
—JACK KETCHUM, author of *The Girl Next Door*

"Carlton Mellick III is one of bizarro fiction's most talented practitioners, a virtuoso of the surreal, science fictional tale."
—CORY DOCTOROW, author of *Little Brother*

"Bizarre, twisted, and emotionally raw—Carlton Mellick's fiction is the literary equivalent of putting your brain in a blender."
—BRIAN KEENE, author of *The Rising*

"Carlton Mellick III exemplifies the intelligence and wit that lurks between its lurid covers. In a genre where crude titles are an art in themselves, Mellick is a true artist."
—*THE GUARDIAN*

"Just as Pop had Andy Warhol and Dada Tristan Tzara, the Bizarro movement has its very own P. T. Barnum-type practitioner. He's the mutton-chopped author of such books as *Electric Jesus Corpse* and *The Menstruating Mall*, the illustrator, editor, and instructor of all things Bizarro, and his name is Carlton Mellick III."
—*DETAILS MAGAZINE*

Also by Carlton Mellick III

ARMADILLO FISTS

CARLTON MELLICK III

ERASERHEAD PRESS
PORTLAND, OREGON

ERASERHEAD PRESS
205 NE BRYANT
PORTLAND, OR 97211

WWW.ERASERHEADPRESS.COM

ISBN: 1-62105-015-7

AUTHOR'S NOTE

First it was vampires. Then it was serial killers. Then it was zombies. Now they're saying it's werewolves. But you know what I think the next big thing in horror literature will be?

Dinosaurs.

Fucking hell yeah I said dinosaurs. What did you think I was going to say? Mummies? Fuck mummies. Dinosaurs are going to take over. And who the hell wouldn't want to read hundreds of dinosaur horror books? Come on, there's a million things you could do with them: people traveling back in time to fight dinosaurs, dinosaurs traveling forward in time to eat people, dinosaurs from space, dinosaurs with lasers, dinosaur mummies. The list could go on forever.

Since I was anticipating this big dinosaur horror wave, I decided to already tweak the genre clichés before the clichés have even been established yet. For starters, my dinosaur horror book isn't even horror. It is closer to the gangster genre than horror, like one of those "on the run from the mob" kind of stories. And it doesn't actually have any dinosaurs in it. The dinosaurs are just giant robotic motor vehicles that are shaped like dinosaurs. How fucking clever is that?

Actually, now that I think about it, this book wouldn't work at all for fans of the upcoming dinosaur horror trend. I better get to work on a real dinosaur book soon. How about I write a sequel to *Apeshit* and throw some random dinosaurs in it? Maybe that could work . . .

I think my favorite way to write a book these days is to come up with the dumbest idea I can possibly think of—you know, like an ex-boxer with armadillos for hands is on the run from the mob in a world where people drive giant mechanical dinosaurs instead of cars—and then approach the book with complete sincerity and put all of my heart into it. I believe all of my best works have been created this way. I even cried while I was writing *The Faggiest Vampire.*

Armadillo Fists is one of my favorite books I've written in the recent past. I think the cast of characters is what does it for me. June and Tony are two of my favorite heroes I've ever written. And I like the villains even better than the heroes.

This is the first time I've ever experimented with plotting in a non-linear fashion. I'm normally not a fan of plots that bounce around too much. In the end, it proved to be a lot of fun and I don't believe this story would have worked if approached in any other way. I don't think I'll write another book without a linear plot, but it worked for me this time.

So I hope you enjoy this book as much as I enjoyed writing it. It's not dinosaur horror, alas, but hopefully you'll like it even better. I'll save dinosaur horror for another time.

—Carlton Mellick III 12/6/2011, 4:04 am

This book is dedicated to Moon Kana, Tite Kubo, Jordan Krall and Quentin Tarantino, for influencing this book whether I wanted them to or not.

CHAPTER ONE

"You're heavy for a man with no arms or legs," June said to Tony as she dragged him across the warehouse floor.

Tony didn't respond. He wasn't conscious. Blood dribbled from his nose and ears. The four stumps where his arms and legs should have been were limp, dangling from his torso like wet sausages.

June couldn't feel his heartbeat when she checked for a pulse. But that didn't mean he was necessarily dead. She's had a very weak sense of touch ever since she replaced her hands with living armadillos.

"You can't die on me now," she said to him, her armadillo hands wrapped around his stumps, gripping him as tightly as they possibly could with such tiny limbs. "Not after all of this."

The fire was growing around them, curling up the walls, swallowing all of their exits. The whole place could collapse on top of them at any minute. If only he wasn't so heavy. If only she was just a little stronger. If only she had real hands.

Her armadillo fingers slid off of his stumps and he plopped down onto the concrete, beer belly wiggling as it fell out of his spandex shirt. There were three charred bullet holes on the side of his stomach.

"Damn these hands," she cried to the armadillos attached to her wrists.

The armadillos blinked up at her, squirming inside their shells like babies in armored cradles. One of them licked its nose with a long sticky tongue.

The south wall exploded. Flaming bits of wood scattered across the warehouse floor. Then a large man emerged from the fire, dragging a slab of concrete.

"He's still alive?" June whispered to Tony, as she saw the hulk of a man stomping toward them.

9

The man's eyes, as red as the fire around him, were locked on June. He raised the concrete slab over his shoulder like a hammer. The man didn't appear human to June. The red eyes, the spiked iron mask covering his face, the horrible cavernous scars covering his massive chest; he was like a demonic executioner. Even with the long metal stakes impaled between his ribs and stomach, he was still walking. The black blood leaking down his muscles only made him look more ferocious.

June stepped forward and curled her armadillo hands into balls. Then she raised her fists and got into a boxing stance.

"You want to go again?" she asked the hulk, ash and cinders raining onto her shoulders like snowflakes. "Let's go. Round two."

She hopped from side to side, her feet dancing as the fire raged around them. She swung her armadillo fists into the air like boxing gloves, taking a few practice swings before the monstrous man came into range.

"You know, I've never lost a match," she said in a stuttering voice, talking more to herself than the metal-faced man. "I'm an undefeated champion!"

But as the hulk stomped closer to her, she found herself inching away from him. With her eyes focused on the slab of concrete, she didn't notice the corpse on the ground behind her. She tripped and fell back, landing next to the body. At first, she thought she had tripped over Tony. But it wasn't him. It was the corpse of a guy named Mr. Happy.

The dead man was wearing a bright yellow suit and yellow hat. He had a bullet in his forehead and a smile on his face. June knew she had to get up before the man in the metal mask crushed her skull with his concrete club, but she couldn't look away from Mr. Happy. The smile on his cold dead face unnerved her, made her armadillos squirm in their shells.

His name was Mr. Happy for a good reason. Even death didn't stop him from smiling.

CHAPTER TWO

Mr. Happy was smiling when he heard the news.

"The boss is really dead?" asked the fat guy, standing in the middle of the group next to Mr. Happy. He had two Chicago-style hot dogs in each hand, taking bites between sentences, bright green relish spilling onto his man-breasts. "I thought that son of a bitch was immortal."

When he said *son of a bitch*, Mr. Happy looked at him. Then the fat guy bit his tongue. He had forgotten that Mr. Happy was the boss' nephew. But Mr. Happy was not upset by his words. He was happy. Always happy. Even the news of his beloved uncle's death, who meant the world to him, would not alter his blissful mood.

Mr. Happy turned back to the old guy at the front of the room and asked, "What happened to him?"

"Murdered," the old guy said, wiping sweat from his crooked forehead. "Armadillo Fists killed him."

"The boxer broad?" asked the fat guy. "Psycho June Howard?"

The old man screwed up his lips and spit tobacco juice onto the carpet. It was his way of saying *yes*. Then he said, "Come with me."

As the group of men followed the old guy down the hall-way, Mr. Happy asked him, "Why'd she do it?"

"How the fuck would I know why she did it," the old man said. "She's a crazy bitch. How's that for an answer?"

The old guy was an asshole when he was on edge. And he was always on edge. They didn't call him *Rape Face* because he was a pleasant person to be around.

They arrived at their boss' personal gym at the end of the hallway. As old Rape Face opened the door, he said, "All I know is, the boss is dead."

The men looked into the room to see their boss' body lying

on the floor. His skull was smashed into bloody chunks, spread across a wrestling mat.

"And we're going after the bitch who killed him," Rape Face said.

Mr. Happy stared at his uncle's mangled corpse, smiling. He hoped the dead body would make him feel sadness or anger. But, like always, the sight only made him happy.

"Steve and Mr. Slick are already on her tail," Rape Face told the crew, rubbing a large white burn scar on the tip of his nose. "We need to catch up to them."

He pointed at Mr. Happy, the fat guy, and a tall, lanky man standing behind them. "Mr. Happy, Mr. Food, Mr. Marathon, you're taking the triceratops."

Then he turned to a dark-haired, nicely-dressed man with rectangular glasses and piercing eyes. "Mr. Sorry, you're with me in the T-rex."

"Can't we take the titanosaur?" asked Mr. Food, stuffing his last Chicago dog in his mouth. "It's more comfortable."

"It's too slow," said Rape Face. To the last three men standing in the hall, he said, "The rest of you, take care of the boss' body." He pointed at a muscular man with a number six tattooed around his left eye. "Call a mortician or something. Get it out of here before his fucking kids come home for fuck's sake."

The man with the tattooed eye nodded and took two guys with him back toward the boss' body. Then Rape Face opened a weapons closet and started handing guns to Mr. Sorry and Mr. Happy.

"You sure we need all of this, Face?" asked Mr. Marathon. "It's just one woman. I mean, we probably don't even need to go. Slick and Steve could take care of her themselves."

"She's not alone," said Rape Face. "Mr. Torso is helping her."

"You mean the amputee?" asked Marathon.

Mr. Food laughed.

Rape Face spit tobacco juice.

"Come on," said Mr. Food, "the guy's got no arms or legs. How's he going to be a problem?"

Mr. Food's chuckles were cut short when Mr. Sorry's cold eyes glared into him.

"Torso is not somebody to be underestimated," said Mr. Sorry in his monotone voice. "Armless, legless, it doesn't matter. When he's behind the wheel, he's the deadliest man on the road."

Rape Face spit more tobacco juice. Then he said, "He's the best driver we've ever had."

CHAPTER THREE

"How's it going, Long Legs?" Tony said to June with a wink and smile as she walked down the boss' driveway.

She wasn't in the mood for Tony's usual routine. The boss had put her in a bad mood that day.

"Just give me a ride home," she said, wiping sweat from her tattooed stomach using the armadillos' shells instead of the towel wrapped around her neck. "I'm tired."

Her words didn't deter him. Tony was a wild cat on the prowl. He only saw it as a challenge. He put on a pair of designer sunglasses with his arm-stumps, as if he were thinking *time to get serious.*

"How about we go for a drink first, Sexy Mamma?" When he spoke his head bobbed side to side, and a sly grin crossed his lips.

Even though he had no arms or legs, Tony always thought of himself as the coolest guy in the universe. He strutted smoothly up the driveway toward her, walking on his stumps like tiny, dwarf-like legs.

"Not today, Mr. Torso," she said. She knew he hated being called Mr. Torso.

He struck a pose and aimed an arm-stump at her, as if pointing. "I think you've got me confused with somebody else, babe. The name's not Mr. Torso. It's *Mr. Awesome.*"

Then he slicked his hair back with the side of his arm-stump, lowered his sunglasses and winked.

June never understood how this half-a-man could have so much confidence. Not only was he missing his limbs at the knees and elbows, but he wasn't even that good-looking otherwise. His eyes were too far apart, he was out of shape, his beer belly hung out of a hideous neon-orange spandex shirt, his chest was too hairy, and his surfer hairstyle wasn't nearly as suave as he thought it was.

June groaned and said in a snarky tone, "Because you're so awesome, eh?"

Although June's freakish armadillo hands usually scared away most sleazy guys trying to pick her up, they did not bother Tony in the slightest. He liked her legs and her ass and made a point to regularly compliment her on them. Her hands could have been cow patties for all he cared.

"I just want to go home, take a shower, and forget all about today," June said.

Tony patted her on the thigh with his stump. "Sounds like you could use a drink to me."

"I could use a nap," she said.

He bobbed his head. "Come on, baby. The drinks are on me. Let Mr. Awesome show you a good time."

June could tell by the amputee's aggressive stance that this time he wasn't going to take no for an answer.

June had to use both of her armadillo hands to lift the beer to her lips. Their bellies were extra sensitive to the cold glass. When she set the beer down, the armadillos rubbed their legs together to warm themselves.

"How can you work for that asshole?" Tony asked her.

He could tell by the look in her eyes that the boss was putting her through hell.

"You work for him, too."

"Yeah," Tony said, "but I'm just his driver. I don't really have to interact with the guy that much."

The waitress in the purple leather dress looked at June funny as she gave them another round of beers. At first, June thought it was because she was still in her sweaty boxing clothes, but then she realized it had to have been her weird hands.

As June went for her fresh beer, the armadillos kicked the glass away and it toppled over, spilling across the table. She lowered her head and groaned.

"Do they have names?" Tony asked, nodding toward her armadillos as they licked at the beer puddle.

She laughed. The question caught her off guard.

"Actually, they do." She raised her right fist and the armadillo squirmed in the air. "This one is Jocko." She raised her left fist, which promptly curled into a ball. "This one is Judy."

"So one's a boy and one's a girl?"

"They don't really have reproductive systems, so I don't know what their genders actually are. But that's how I view them."

June brushed her bangs out of her face. Jocko tried to chew her hair as it slid across his chin.

"They seem to have minds of their own," Tony said, drinking from a beer held by both of his stump-arms.

"They do," June said. "I can control them just as if they were a part of my body, but when I relax them they'll move around on their own. It's a difficult sensation to explain. They're a part of me, yet sometimes they're like pets. They have their own personalities."

"Do you have to feed them?"

"They would try to eat if I'd let them, but then they'd just puke it up. They don't have digestive systems anymore. My body supplies them with nutrients."

"Like babies in their mother's womb?"

"Something like that."

"Where'd you get them attached? You couldn't have been born that way . . ."

"I had to go to another world to get it done," June said. "One of my dops convinced me to do it."

Tony's eyes lit up. "You've gone to a Dop Convention?"

June nodded.

"I just went last month," Tony said.

"How were your dops?"

"They were all awesome, you know," he said, bobbing his head. "Just like me."

He leaned his stump against the table, right in the middle

of the puddle of beer. "I think everyone should go to their Dop Convention. It really changed my life forever."

June sighed and looked down at her armadillo hands.

"Tell me about it," she said.

CHAPTER FOUR

A Dop Convention is kind of like a high school reunion, but instead of connecting with old school friends the point is to meet different versions of yourself from alternate dimensions. These other versions of yourself are called dops, or *doppelgangers*.

The June Howard Convention took place four years ago. June didn't really want to go to her Dop Convention. She didn't like the idea of meeting other versions of herself. She'd heard the horror stories about how esteem-crushing they could be. If all of the other June Howards were prettier, wealthier, and more successful than she was it would make her feel like an even bigger loser than she already was.

"But you *have* to go to your Dop Convention," one of her friends told her, a week before the event. "It's a once in a life-time experience!"

Another friend said, "If the other Junes are more successful than you then you should take it as inspiration. It will show you how much potential you truly have!"

"But whatever you do, don't lez-out with any of the other versions of you," another friend said, giggling. "We know you're bi-curious, but that would just be *wrong.*"

June ignored their laughs, busy reconsidering whether she should go or not.

"Could you imagine being in a room full of June Howards?" her friends said to each other, as if June couldn't hear them. "It'd be *so* boring."

Another friend said, "They'd all just stand there staring at each other."

"They'd just smoke pot and watch television."

"They'd just hang around in sweat pants, belching and farting at each other."

"They're probably all fat."

"They'd probably hate each other."

"They'd probably get drunk and then try to fight each other."

"Then they'd lez-out!"

"They'd totally lez-out!"

"The hotel would become a huge orgy of lesbian June Howards!"

The girls giggled and looked at June.

"You *have* to go, June," they said. "You're going to have so much fun!"

That's when June decided to go to her Dop Convention. She hated her life, hated her job, and really hated her friends, and she wanted to see if the other Junes felt the same way. She wanted to meet the other versions of herself just to see if there wasn't anything she could have done differently, anything she could have done to have made her life worthwhile.

At first, she was nervous about being the biggest loser of all the June Howards. But then she realized the absolute worse case scenario would be if they were even bigger losers than she was.

June decided to look good for her convention. She might not have been the most feminine girl she knew, but she was in really good shape. She took Tae Bo classes. She was always at the gym lifting weights and would run five miles a day. She also loved boxing. Although she never actually sparred with anyone, there was something about pounding the shit out of a punching bag that made her feel better about herself. It was how she released all the aggression that built up in her during her shitty 9 to 5 call center job.

So she got a new haircut: short in the back, long in the front. Her friends always called this hairstyle a reverse-mullet, but June liked it. She painted her nails camouflage, wore combat boots, a short green-plaid skirt, and half-shirt that exposed her tattooed stomach. She got her lips and eyebrows pierced. If she wasn't going to be the most successful June Howard, at least she was going to be the toughest. Maybe she'd even frighten the other versions of herself a little. That would make her feel better, especially if they were a bunch of snobs.

When June arrived at the inter-dimensional hotel where the convention was to be held, she thought she had walked into the wrong meeting hall. It said "June Howard Doppelganger Convention" outside the door, but inside she didn't see anybody that looked like her. In fact, the room was filled with a bunch of guys.

When she realized that she was indeed in the correct location, she wanted to smash her head against the wall.

"Shit, they're all *men* . . ." she said. "All of the other versions of me are men . . ."

She couldn't believe her eyes. She was in a room full of male versions of herself. Most of them were muscular, handsome men in nice clothing. A lot of them looked like football players. They were laughing with each other, patting each other on the back like old friends. Whereas June was more introverted, these guys seemed extroverted and charismatic. Alpha males. The type of guys who would be the life of the party.

June needed a drink. She rushed through the crowd to the bar. More than one of the male June Howards checked out her ass as she passed by.

She shook her head. Her friends were going to tease her relentlessly if they ever found out that the other June Howards were men.

At the bar, she slammed a Scotch whiskey. She didn't recognize the brand; it was probably from another dimension. It tasted like shit but got the job done.

"So there *is* another lady June?" said a gruff voice to her right. She turned to see a large, muscular woman standing next to her. The woman looked like what June would have looked like if she had taken steroids her whole life and wore her hair in a long pony tail. Next to Muscle June was a girl in a wheelchair. Her face was wrinkled and withered. Her eyes were deep in their sockets. Her breasts were saggy. She looked like what June would have looked like had she become a heroin addict.

"We thought we were the only ones," said Wheelchair June.

June looked at them and said, "Why are all the others guys?"

Muscle June said, "Yeah, it kind of freaked me out as well, at first. It means that we were *supposed* to have been born guys, but some little mix up while we were in the womb changed our destiny. They say it happens all the time."

"But why were we given a girl's name if we were supposed to be guys?" June asked.

"I don't know what you're talking about," Muscle June said. "Where I come from, June is a boy's name. I was ridiculed my whole life."

"It's mostly a girl's name in my world," said Wheelchair June.

"Mine too," June said.

"Well, either way," Muscle June said, taking a deep breath, "the three of us are the female June Howards. We should be proud." Then Muscle June smiled at June. "Especially you."

"Me?"

"Yeah, you're the cutest June Howard in the room," said Muscle June. Then she winked.

June realized Muscle June was flirting with her. She instantly heard her friends' voices in her head, saying, "They'd totally lez-out!" and she suddenly became nervous.

"I, uhhh . . ." she said, trying to think of a way to change the topic.

But Muscle June changed it for her. "So what do you do for a living?"

June shrugged. "Just a call center job. Lately, I've been struggling with trying to figure out what I want to do with my life."

"Oh, I've always known what I wanted to do with my life," said Muscle June.

"What's that?"

Muscle June held up her fists. "I wanted to be a boxer. So that's exactly what I became."

June's eyes lit up. "I *love* boxing. I totally could see myself pursuing boxing in another life."

Then June noticed something strange about Muscle June's fists. They were hard gray balls that looked kind of like rocks or turtle shells.

"What's with your hands?" June asked.

"These are my boxing mitts," said Muscle June. Then her hands unfolded into armadillos. Their legs squirmed in the air at her.

"Armadillos? Attached to your hands?"

"I'm surprised you didn't notice right away." Muscle June chuckled. "In my world, all boxers implant armadillos on their fists. It's part of the sport's tradition. You wouldn't believe how much harder you throw punches with these babies."

Right then, June realized how envious she was of her muscular doppelganger. She had always wanted to be a boxer her whole life, but only at that moment did she realize it.

"I want to be a boxer," June said.

Muscle June smiled, pleased to have inspired another version of herself. She said, "If you can ever afford an inter-dimensional passport come visit me in my world. I'll give you a few pointers."

"Thanks," June said.

"Not only that, but I'll hook you up with a doctor who could give you the operation." She held up her armadillo fists. "With these bad boys hidden beneath your boxing gloves, you'd become a champ in no time."

June shook her head and waved her hands. "No, thank you . . . I think I'll play by the rules."

She couldn't imagine what it would be like to cut off her hands and replace them with living animals.

"Suit yourself," said Muscle June. "The offer still stands."

June cringed at the sight of the armadillos curled in the muscular woman's lap. "Thanks . . ."

"So what do you do?" June asked Wheelchair June.

"I used to be a dancer before the accident," says Wheelchair June, looking down at her legs.

"How'd it happen?"

"A car accident," she said. "I work late hours and fell asleep while driving home. My Lexus hit a parked car and I was thrown through the windshield."

"What's a Lexus?" June asked.

"It's a kind of car in my world."

"What's a car?" June asked.

Both Muscle June and Wheelchair June looked at her funny.

"You don't have cars in your world?" asked Wheelchair June. June shook her head.

"If you don't drive cars, then what do you use for transportation in your world?" Muscle June asked.

"We drive dinosaurs," June said.

"Dinosaurs?" asked Wheelchair June. "Like the extinct animals? Like the Flintstones?"

Neither June nor Muscle June knew what *Flintstones* meant.

"No, not real dinosaurs," June said. "They're machines shaped like dinosaurs."

June dug through her bag for a pop culture magazine. Then she flipped through the pages until she found a picture example of one of her world's vehicles.

"Like this one," June said, holding up the magazine for them to see.

The two alternate versions of June inspected the image closely. They saw a metal hadrosaur as large as a real hadrosaur. Just like cars from their worlds, the mechanical dinosaur had doors, seats, a dashboard, and a hood ornament. The interior looked very similar to the interiors of vehicles from their worlds. But the exterior looked like a dinosaur-shaped robot.

"How fast do they go?" asked Muscle June.

"Pretty fast," June said. "It depends on the dinosaur. Some

of them can get up to two hundred miles per hour."

"Two hundred!" said Muscle June. "In that thing?"

"Probably not this one," June said, "but in a triceratops, yeah."

"What happened in your world's history that caused you to drive mechanical dinosaurs instead of cars?"

June shrugged. "I have no idea why you people *don't* drive mechanical dinosaurs."

"You don't think it's weird that your vehicles are dinosaur-shaped?"

"A long time ago, we used to ride horses for transportation," June said. "Then we rode elephants, moose, giraffe, and all kinds of animals. Eventually, we switched to riding mechanical animals instead of living animals. Then we started riding mechanical dinosaurs instead of animals, because they're bigger and usually faster. Some time before I was born, we started riding inside of the machines instead of outside. It was a pretty logical transition."

"Haven't your people ever heard of the wheel?" asked Wheelchair June.

"Yeah," June said.

"Then why don't you build vehicles with wheels instead of legs?"

"Like on wheelchairs and shopping carts?" June laughed. "Legs are better than wheels. How would you be able to drive through snow or get over rocky terrain without legs on your vehicles? How do you jump over other vehicles that are driving too slow? How do you drive sideways?"

The two women shook their heads, not able to fathom what June was talking about.

"You live in a totally different world than we do, Dinosaur June," said Muscle June. "Totally different world."

Then Muscle June took a sip of her martini, holding the glass awkwardly with her armadillo hands.

CHAPTER FIVE

June ran out of the boss' house toward Tony's mechanical stegosaurus. It's the dinosaur Tony usually drove their boss around in.

When Tony looked up from an issue of *Babes & Dinos* magazine, he could tell something was wrong. June had a black eye, her nose was bleeding, and her lips were swollen.

"You've got to help me," June said to Tony, leaning against the side of the stegosaurus, trying to catch her breath.

"What's wrong, Sugar Legs?"

She jumped into the passenger seat.

"Just drive," she said. "Get me out of here!"

With his right stump-arm, he popped the gear shift into drive and then lowered his sunglasses over his eyes.

"Sure thing, babydoll," Tony said, bobbing his head with excitement. "Anything for you."

The stegosaurus walked slowly down the steel driveway, its spiked tail swinging back and forth.

"Faster!" June said, looking back over her shoulder at the boss' front door.

"You want to go *fast?*" Tony turned to her and raised his eyebrows over the rims of his sunglasses. "You've come to the right place. They don't call me Mr. *Fast* Awesome for nothing."

"Nobody calls you that!" June yelled. "Just drive!"

After her words, the stegosaurus leapt out of the driveway and slid across the steel surface of the street. Then Tony shoved his leg-stump into the gas pedal extension, custom designed for his stubby legs, and accelerated to top speed.

June's head slammed back into the headrest as the stegosaurus galloped down the street. Then the sound of bullets ricocheting off of metal filled their ears.

"What the hey?" Tony said, looking in the rearview mirror. "Somebody's shooting at us!"

"Just drive," June said.

The stegosaurus turned the corner, then the next corner, escaping the gunfire.

"What the hell happened back there?" Tony asked her.

"I killed the boss."

"What!"

"I fucking killed him," she said. "And if you don't help me they're going to kill me, too."

Tony went silent. It was the first time June had ever seen a serious look on his face. June was worried that he was going to turn the dino around and give her up to Rape Face and the others.

"We'll take the south highway out of town," Tony said. His voice sounded unfamiliar to June. It was calm, calculating. He sounded like a completely different person. "It will have the least traffic."

"You're going to help me?" June asked.

Tony didn't answer her.

He said, "They'll probably send one dino after us right away. If we can shake that one, we'll probably be alright. But within the hour, I'm sure Rape Face will get all of his best guys together and send them after us. They're not going to let us go so easily."

"*Us?*" June asked.

Tony looked at her.

"Yeah," he said. "You killed my employer, Sugar Legs. I don't have any reason to stick around this town anymore."

Then the stegosaurus hopped over an ankylosaurus, then over a guard rail, and onto the freeway.

CHAPTER SIX

Tony never really liked the boss, but he appreciated the pay-checks and the perks of the job. He met the guy on a pterosaur while flying across country. Tony was sitting next to him on the aircraft. He felt kind of bad for the guy. The old man was shaking so hard the ice cubes rattled in his whiskey tonic.

"You okay, my man?" Tony said, patting him on the shoulder with an arm-stump.

"I fucking hate these flights," he said to Tony. He guzzled down the last of his drink and then started sucking on the ice cubes to absorb every last drop of alcohol he could. "The god damned thing bounces up and down too much."

Tony looked past him out of the window. The metal wings of the pterosaur flapped slowly through the air. It was a sight that made many pterosaur passengers nauseous.

"Here," Tony said, pulling out a plastic retractable baton. In one swift motion, he took the baton in his mouth, extended it with a whip of his neck, slammed the window blinder down with its tip, retracted it, and slid it back into his coat. "It's better when you don't have to look out the window."

Tony didn't realize he had also knocked the drink out of the old guy's hand.

"What the fuck, you freak?" the old guy said.

"Sorry, my man," Tony said. "Just trying to help."

The old guy glared at the amputee. He was a broad-shouldered man with very little hair on his overly large head. His flesh was saggy and covered in liver spots, but Tony could tell that beneath the wrinkled skin the guy was all muscle.

"Hey, don't I know you?" asked the old man.

Tony shrugged.

"You're that NASDAR driver from television," he said to Tony. NASDAR stood for *National Association for Stock Dino-*

saur Auto Racing. "The racer who won the Tricera-Cup Series with no arms or legs?"

"That would be me," Tony said.

"Well, holy Jesus," the old guy said. Then he made a loud hacking noise that was somewhere between a laugh and a cough. "You were pretty damned good."

"I was better than good," Tony said, bobbing his head with pride.

The old guy offered him his hand. "The name's Bobby Mazetti. My friends call me Big Bob."

"Tony Kudrow," Tony said.

"Yeah, I know."

Tony didn't have a hand to shake with, so he offered him a stump. Big Bob cough-laughed when he shook the stubby limb.

While the old guy's arm was extended, Tony saw a gun hanging out of his coat. He wondered what he was doing with a gun on a pterosaur. He could tell that the guy was no air marshal. The gun was special, made from an ultra-dense plastic. It was designed to be carried through airport metal detectors, but still strong enough to kill a man as quickly as a .38 Special. Tony knew right away that this guy had to have been a wealthy, dangerous man. But the sight of the gun didn't unhinge Tony. The amputee wasn't afraid of anyone.

"So, you still racing?" Big Bob asked.

Tony let out a long sigh. "Actually, not anymore. They dropped me last February."

"Those motherfuckers!" Big Bob yelled loud enough that everyone on the pterosaur could hear him. Tony had no idea why the guy would be so upset about the news. He assumed the man was a little drunk. "Why'd they do that? You were damned good."

Tony shrugged. "Ever since the incident with the Governor's daughter, sponsors didn't want to have anything to do with me."

Big Bob paused for a minute and then burst into laughter. "Oh yeah! I forgot all about that. That was you, huh? Getting caught diddling the Governor's daughter in a parked spinosaurus! You legless son of a bitch, that was hilarious."

"Not really," Tony said. "After it was all over the tabloids, it killed my career."

But Big Bob didn't seem to hear him. He was laughing so close to Tony's face that he thought the old bastard was going to French kiss his ear.

"I like you, kid," Big Bob said, patting him on the shoulder. "You've got my kind of man seed."

"Man seed?"

"So what are you doing these days?" Bob asked.

"Not much," Tony said. "I'm just living off the last of my savings."

"How about you come work for me?" Bob asked. "I could use a guy with your kind of talents."

"What kind of work?"

"Driving," Bob said. "You know, odd jobs. But it's good pay. Tax free."

Tony smirked.

"I'll think about it," he said, rubbing his neck with an arm-stump. "I'll definitely think about it."

CHAPTER SEVEN

"What's that on your neck?" June asked Tony as they drove down the freeway in the stegosaurus.

She was pointing at the tattoo of the number eight on his neck.

"Oh, this?" Tony asked, rubbing the tattoo with his stump. "Big Bob made me get it."

"I've seen them on some of the other guys," she said. "What's it for?"

"It's how Big Bob ranks his men in order of toughness. Number one's the most badass guy in his organization. I'm number eight because I'm the eighth biggest badass who works for him." He bobbed his head with a touch of pride.

June said, "I saw the number seven tattooed on the back of another guy's hand, the smiley guy who always wears the yellow suits."

"Yeah, Mr. Happy. He's the seventh biggest badass. Rape Face is number nine, even though he thinks he's number one."

"Was Big Bob number one?" June asked.

"No, he didn't give himself a number. I guess he was zero."

"Then who's number one?"

Before Tony could respond, the sound of a bullet ricocheting off of one of the stegosaurus' plates caused them both to jump.

"Fuck," Tony said, driving into the next lane of the freeway. "They caught up to us sooner than I expected."

June looked back to see a dimetrodon galloping down the freeway at top speed, heading straight for them.

"It's Magic Steve," Tony said. "Don't worry. The guy's an idiot. He can't drive for shit."

Tony slammed on the gas and his stegosaurus charged forward, leaping sideways over two old ladies in iguanodons. He drove alongside the iguanodons, using them as a barrier between the stegosaurus and the dimetrodon.

Bullets tore into the back of the stegosaurus. Somehow, they were able to get through the iguanodon barrier.

"How are they hitting us?" June asked.

Tony looked back at the man in black firing at them from the passenger side window.

"Fuck," Tony said. "Slick is riding with Magic Steve."

"Slick?" June asked.

"You know how I'm ranked number eight?" Tony said.

"Yeah?"

"Well, Mr. Slick is number five."

"Is that bad?" June asked.

"Real bad," Tony said.

His arm-stump pushed June's head below the dashboard as a shower of bullets broke through the back window.

When the firing ceased, Tony said, "It could have been a lot worse, though. It could have been Mr. Sorry."

CHAPTER EIGHT

Black tears rolled down Mr. Sorry's cheeks as he and Rape Face drove the T-rex down the freeway.

"What, are you crying over there again?" Rape Face said.

Mr. Sorry's tears were always black. He didn't know why. Doctors couldn't explain it. There wasn't a scientific explanation for the coloration or why they dribbled out randomly, multiple times a day.

His mother used to say his tears were black because he didn't have a soul. It was the alcoholic bitch's idea of a joke. As a result, Mr. Sorry spent most of his childhood believing that he didn't have a soul and it colored his personality accordingly.

The tears were like squid ink, so Mr. Sorry always wore black. Any other colored clothing would be ruined every time he cried. He wiped the tears away. The black ink was even darker than his black leather gloves. Then he flicked the liquid out the window, from the passenger seat inside the T-rex's head.

"Motherfuckers," Rape Face said. He was in an ugly mood.

As he drove, Rape Face hit the speaker phone on the dashboard.

"Yeah?" Mr. Food answered on the other line.

"Fuck, put Happy on the phone, would ya?" Rape Face yelled at the top of his lungs. He didn't realize that Food could hear him just fine.

"I'll put you on speaker," Food said.

Happy's voice came on the line. Even though Sorry and Rape Face couldn't see him, they could hear his smile stretching from ear to ear.

"Yes, Mr. Face?" Happy asked.

"Have you heard from Steve and Slick?" Rape Face asked him.

"No," Happy said.

"Motherfucker!" said Rape Face.

"What's that?"

"Nothing," Rape Face said. "Go to Canyon Road. That's the last time we heard from them."

"Sure, boss," Happy said.

"That idiot Steve better not have fucked this up," said Rape Face.

"See you there, boss," Happy said.

"Yeah, see ya there, ya fuck."

There was a pause for a moment. The passengers in Happy's triceratops thought Rape Face had turned off his phone, but Mr. Sorry and Rape Face could still hear them on the line.

"Why'd you call Rape Face *boss*?" Mr. Food asked Mr. Happy, unaware that the speaker phone was still on.

"At this moment, he's the one in charge," said Happy.

"You think that Rape Face is going to take over the organization now that the boss is dead?" asked Mr. Food.

"Probably."

"Fuck, that's going to suck. Rape Face is such a douchebag."

Mr. Sorry could tell Rape Face was getting pissed off as he listened in on their conversation. The asshole didn't speak up, though, just stewed quietly.

"Why do they call him *Rape Face* anyway?" asked Mr. Marathon.

"Are you kidding me?" said Mr. Food. "Have you ever looked at that guy's face? He's got *rapist* written all over him."

"Like his facial expression is the same as someone who's about to rape a woman?" asked Mr. Marathon

"No, it's the facial expression of someone who's about to rape *ten* women."

Mr. Sorry could hear Rape Face's teeth grinding in his mouth.

"Like someone with a rape fetish?"

"Like someone on a raping spree."

"Like somebody who's going to rape everything in his path?"

"Like how sharks go on into a feeding frenzy, he looks like

he's going on a raping frenzy."

Then they laughed. Mr. Sorry could tell Rape Face had enough.

"Your phone's still on, you motherfuckers!" Rape Face yelled.

The men on the other line went silent.

"I'll rape you with a bullet up your asses, you fucking good for nothing sons of bitches!"

The men on the other line stayed silent.

Mr. Food slowly hit the *off* button on his phone. They drove in silence for a few minutes.

"Oops," Mr. Food said.

Then he burst into laughter.

Mr. Food was short for *Food Mountain*. He was proud of the nickname. The guy weighed four hundred and fifty pounds and wasn't looking back. He might only have been ranked number ten in the organization, but he wasn't afraid of the guys ranked higher than him. Because he had so many layers of fat on his body, he was good in a fight. No matter how many times he got punched, he couldn't feel a thing.

"You think Rape Face really does rape people?" Mr. Marathon asked.

"Probably," said Mr. Food. "I've never seen him with a girl before. He's got to get his pussy somehow."

"You think he's gay?"

"Nah, I just don't think any bitch would ever go near him. Not unless he paid her. A lot. And knowing that cheap bastard he'd probably become a rapist just to save money."

"Hey," Mr. Marathon said. "Who do you think would have a better chance picking up a girl, Rape Face or Mr. Torso?"

"What, are you kidding me?" said Mr. Food. "Mr. Torso, of course."

"But Torso has no arms or legs. What the hell would he do with a woman?"

"What are you talking about?" said Mr. Food. "Torso is a

fucking ladies man. You ever seen that guy in action? He's got the ladies lined up around the block."

"You serious?"

"Yeah, the guy's buried up to his eyebrows in pussy."

CHAPTER NINE

June lay naked on the hotel room bed, spread eagle, covered in sweat. Her arms stretched out, the armadillo hands dangling off the sides of the bed. Her pale breasts rose and fell on her chest as she tried to catch her breath.

She looked over at Tony's wiggling bare butt as he struggled to pull on his tiny spandex shorts.

"Why was that so damned *good*?" June yelled at him, panting. "It's never been like *that* with anyone before."

"I told you, Sugar Legs," Tony said, leaning against the wall with his stubby arm. "They don't call me *Mr. Awesome* for nothing."

June looked up at the ceiling. She could hardly move.

"How were you able to do that without any arms or legs?" she asked. "It was incredible."

Tony bobbed his head from side to side. "I'm a sex machine, baby. Don't ever forget it."

June closed her eyes and smiled. For a moment, she wanted to forget that they were being hunted by dangerous killers. She wanted to stay in that hotel room bed, wrapped in Tony's arm-stumps, and do nothing but fuck for days.

CHAPTER TEN

Lying in a hospital bed, June looked down at her new hands. The operation had been a success.

"I'm glad you decided to take me up on the offer," Muscle June said to June as she entered the hospital room.

"It feels so strange," June said, sitting up in the bed, rolling and unrolling the armadillos on her wrists.

"You'll get used to it," said Muscle June, holding out her own armadillo fists in a boxing stance.

"I hope I made the right decision," June said.

"Trust me," Muscle June said. "In five months, you'll be knocking out every opponent you go up against."

"Five months?" June asked.

"Yeah, after your wrists heal from the operation."

"What?" June asked. "You mean I have to wait that long before I can fight again?"

"Yeah," said Muscle June.

"But I have a fight next week!"

Muscle June shrugged.

"I don't know what to tell you, Dinosaur June," she said. "If you fight with these next week your hands are going to fall off."

June looked at the armadillos as they crawled across the blanket, trying to get away from her. Instead of giving her the advantage over her opponent, the armadillo fists were going to screw her over.

CHAPTER ELEVEN

The triceratops pulled over on Canyon Road, shining head-lights on the wreckage.

"Look at that," said Mr. Food. "It's totaled."

Mr. Happy got out of the vehicle and stepped over to the dimetrodon. The mechanical dinosaur looked like it had been flattened and tossed to the side of the road. Blood was leaking from the driver's side window. An arm lay in the center of the road.

When Rape Face pulled up behind them in the T-rex, he wasn't happy.

"What the fuck happened here?" said Rape Face, charging at the three men examining the wreckage.

Mr. Happy shook his head at Mr. Face.

"Where's Steve?" Rape Face said. "That asshole's getting my foot up his ass."

Mr. Food popped up from the other side of the wrecked dimetrodon, holding a severed human head.

"Here's his head," said Mr. Food.

Rape Face kicked a metal dinosaur toe across the street. "God damn it!"

"So what should we do now?" asked Mr. Happy.

"How the fuck should I know," Rape Face said, pushing the man in the yellow suit out of his way to examine the wreck-age for himself.

CHAPTER TWELVE

"*RAWWR! RAWWR! RAWWR! RAWWWWWR!*" Magic Steve said, making dinosaur noises as he drove the dimetrodon down the freeway.

He jumped the vehicle over a sluggish ankylosaur and said "WOOOOOOOOOOSH!" as the mechanical dinosaur flew through the air.

When controlling the dinosaur's mouth, he made it bite at the air toward the other dinos on the road, making the sound effects, "CHOMP! CHOMP! CHOMP! RAAAAWWR!"

Mr. Slick sat next to him, glaring at the immature man driving the dino. Slick was a thin, bony man with a shaved head, wearing a black suit and a black hat. His skin was almost as pale as that of an albino's.

When Magic Steve realized that Mr. Slick was glaring at him, he shut his mouth. Then he straightened the red baseball cap on his head. Mr. Slick was not somebody he wanted to annoy. The guy was known to blow people's heads off without warning or hesitation, even people within the organization, even if all they did to piss him off was look at him funny.

After a few minutes of silence, Magic Steve began to shake. He wanted to make more dinosaur noises. He couldn't help himself. Whenever he was in the driver's seat of a dino, he got so excited. He liked to imagine that he actually was a dinosaur living in the age of dinosaurs. He wanted to attack and eat all the other dinosaurs on the road.

"RAWW! RAAWWR! RAAAAAWR!" he said, involuntarily.

When Mr. Slick glared at him again, Magic Steve bit his tongue, using all of his strength to hold his mouth shut. But he couldn't help it.

He whispered to himself, "RAAAAWR... RAAAWR... RAAAWR..."

But Mr. Slick could still hear him. He looked as if he was about to rip Steve's tongue out with a pair of pliers.

"Is that them?" Steve said, before Slick had a chance to do anything to him.

He pointed at the stegosaurus driving a few dinos ahead of them. Slick squinted his eyes to verify it was Mr. Torso's dino. When he had confirmation, he rolled down the window. Then a donut-shaped 9mm handgun whipped out of his suit sleeve into his right hand.

Mr. Slick fired at the stegosaurus, but only hit the plates on its back. When Mr. Torso realized he was being shot at, he jumped his dino to the other side of a couple of iguanodons, using them as shields from the gunfire. But that wasn't going to protect them from Mr. Slick.

"Do your trick," Magic Steve told him. "Shoot around those iguanodons."

Mr. Slick earned his name because of a special shooting technique he used. The handguns that he kept in his sleeves were custom-built. They were not exactly guns. They were more like yo-yos that shot 9mm bullets.

Whipping his hand out of the window, the gun flew two lanes over, past the iguanodons, and fired into the back of the stegosaurus. Then a wire attached to the base of the gun reeled it back into Slick's hand.

As Steve drove them after the stegosaur, Mr. Slick yo-yoed his gun in and out of the window, firing around the backs of dinos, shooting from angles where Mr. Torso couldn't see them coming.

"RAAAWR! RAAAWR! RAAWR!" Magic Steve yelled uncontrollably, as his dimetrodon charged down the street.

The excitement of the chase was too much for him. He couldn't help but make dinosaur noises.

"RAAAAWR! CHOMP! CHOMP! RAAAAWR!"

He imagined himself as a dino on a hunt. He was the powerful carnivore chasing after his herbivore prey.

"CHOMP! CHOMP! CHOMP!"

He couldn't stop himself from biting into the dino in front of him. He drove up behind a slow-moving ouranosaur, who was just trying to get out of their way, and bit into its metal tail. Once it was in the dimetrodon's mouth, Steve thrashed the controller around until the tail was ripped free from the ouranosaur's back.

"CHOMP! CHOMP! RAAAAWR!"

Mr. Slick tried the best he could to ignore the annoying driver as he shot at the stegosaur. As they passed an iguanodon, he could see the old lady driving it, scared out of her mind. She was praying that she wouldn't get hit in the crossfire.

Then Mr. Slick's yo-yo gun flew through the old lady's window and out the other side, shooting at the stegosaur. The old woman screamed at the top of her lungs as the gun went whizzing past her face. The wire was just an inch away from slicing open her throat as it reeled back into Slick's hand.

The stegosaur jumped over the side of the ramp and landed on another freeway running east.

"Holy shit!" Steve yelled. "Did you *see* that?"

As they passed over the eastbound freeway, Mr. Slick tossed his gun over the railing. The wire bent over the bar, sending the gun down to the eastbound freeway below them. It fired into the dinos driving beneath them, but Slick couldn't see where he was shooting. Once they saw the stegosaur driving off into the distance, Slick could tell he didn't land any of his shots.

"After them," said Mr. Slick in a soft whispery voice.

Then Mr. Slick climbed out of the window onto the roof.

Magic Steve took the exit and headed after the stegosaur, growling as he raced through the dino horde.

CHAPTER THIRTEEN

June had difficulty putting her boxing gloves on over the armadillos. They squirmed to escape, clawing at the gloves, trying to dig through them. She had only had them implanted last week, so she was still inexperienced at keeping them under control. They fought against her commands, trying to run free.

She knew Muscle June had told her not to fight for at least five months, but it was her first (and probably only) title shot. She couldn't back out. It was only a fluke that she got the match to begin with. There was no way she was going to cancel. Even if she injured herself, even if she couldn't control the armadillos, even if she lost horribly, she was at least going to try.

After finally stuffing the tiny creatures into the gloves, she looked at herself in the locker room mirror.

"This is your shot, June," she said to her reflection. "Don't fuck it up."

Then she punched her gloves together. The act sent needles of pain up her forearms.

June went down, spitting blood across the mat. Her opponent, the champion Tina Lee, hovered over her. She was dancing over June's body, shaking sweat from her head and punching her gloves together.

But June wasn't out yet. She pulled herself back to her feet. Staggering toward the ropes, her mind was fuzzy. She could barely stand.

"What the heck are you doing out there?" her trainer yelled. "There's no weight behind your punches."

June's hands were in too much pain to throw any real punches. It felt like her fists would break against Tina Lee's face if she tried.

The crowd roared at June. They hated her. They didn't think she deserved to be there. She was still an unknown. And, worst of all, they were bored out of their minds. The announcers just kept repeating, "She's just out of her league," over and over again. June decided she just had to suck up the pain and fight for real.

When the bell dinged, June charged right in. Her balance wasn't very steady, but she fought with all of her strength. Unfortunately, her opponent was just a better boxer than she was. June threw a left, then a right, using all of her strength. But Tina Lee dodged her punches, got in a couple of body blows right below her ribs. The punches hit hard, but the pain was nothing compared to the tearing sensations in her wrists.

While Lee was busy punching her in the stomach again, June threw a left hook at her opponent's jaw. But Lee was too fast. She blocked the punch.

When June's left connected with Lee's block, she heard a loud snap. At first, she didn't see her fist bent all the way back the wrong way. The pain was so intense she went blind for a moment.

Falling to one knee, shrieking, her vision cleared and she saw the armadillo twitching inside her glove. The nerves had been severed. She couldn't control the armadillo in the slightest any more.

Tina Lee's mouth dropped open at the sight of June's broken, squirming fist. She couldn't take her eyes off of it. That's when June saw her opportunity. She launched off of the mat, her right fist aiming at her opponent's face. Lee didn't see the upper cut coming at her. As it connected, Lee was thrown into the air. The audience fell silent. By the time she hit the mat, Lee was already out cold.

The audience cheered. They couldn't believe it. The first punch June actually landed was a knock out punch. The bell dinged. She had won the title. She was a champion. For about two minutes.

June didn't have the strength to stop the medics as they removed her glove, revealing her armadillo hand to everyone. Blood gushed out of June's wrists like a geyser. The armadillo's innards spilled out across the mat. It was dead.

After that night, June was disqualified and barred from boxing ever again. She had to get a new armadillo implanted on her left wrist, only because she didn't know what else to do with the missing hand. She almost didn't get a replacement armadillo, but decided it was worth it. Even if she couldn't fight again, she could still let out her aggression on the punching bag in her free time.

CHAPTER FOURTEEN

Driving down Canyon Road, Tony was able to go faster. The road usually had very little traffic. Any dino they came across, he was able to leap over and continue on with ease.

June kept looking back, wondering if any dino back there was a dimetrodon.

"Think we lost them?" June asked.

"No," Tony said. "They know which way we're headed. For now, all we can hope for is that they don't catch up."

Magic Steve was one with the dimetrodon. He could smell herbivore meat on the road. He was getting close to his prey.

"RAAAAWR! ROOOOAAWR!"

He was able to make dino noises as loud as he wanted with Mr. Slick on the roof.

"RAAAAWR! Chomp! Chomp!"

Making the noises helped Steve get into the zone. When he felt as if he were one with the dinosaur, he was able to drive faster. Maybe even faster than Mr. Torso.

"RAAAAAAAWR!"

When the stegosaur came into his sights, Steve's expression became serious. His eyes were hungry. A quiet growl under his breath. He was a predator on the hunt. He would not allow his prey to escape this time.

Tony saw the dimetrodon closing in behind him.

"Hold on," he told June.

The stegosaur sped up, but wasn't quick enough. The dimetrodon was at their tail. Bullets pierced the metal body around them. Tony looked back at the man standing on the roof of the dimetrodon. He was gripping the sail on the dimetrodon's back, shooting at them with both yo-yo guns at once.

Mr. Slick whipped his arms out and both guns flew on their wires at the stegosaur, one on each side. The guns fired up the sides of the dino, shredding its metal frame.

June screamed and ducked under the dashboard as the bullets shattered the passenger side window.

The dimetrodon bit into the back of the stegosaur, slowing it down. Even over the loud dino engines, Tony could hear Magic Steve yelling *CHOMP! CHOMP! CHOMP!*

Mr. Slick swung one yo-yo gun in a wide arc. When it came at the dino, the gun entered through June's window. Tony pulled her down as the yo-yo gun fired above their heads, hovering in midair within the cab of the vehicle.

After the gun left the window, returning to Slick's hand, June shrieked, "What the fuck was that?"

"I told you Mr. Slick was dangerous," Tony said.

"And there are four more people in the organization more dangerous than him?" June screamed.

"That's right, Sugar Legs," Tony said in a dismissive voice, trying to focus on the road. "Each one is more deadly than the last."

"How the hell are we going to get away from these guys?"

"Don't worry, baby," Tony said, turning to her with a wink. "You've got Mr. Awesome on your side."

Tony swung the spiked stegosaurus tail at the dimetrodon, smacking it away from his rear end. Then he used the opportunity to gain speed.

Up ahead, a large brachiosaurus was driving casually down the road. It was a one lane highway, so Tony had to pass it on the left.

As they passed, June looked up at the driver. He was falling asleep at the controls. Like most sauropod-drivers, he had probably been driving nonstop for the past twenty hours, trying to get his cargo to its destination on time. For a moment, she wished she was riding in a dinosaur that big. She would feel a lot safer sitting all the way up there, beyond where Mr. Slick's yo-yo guns could reach.

The dimetrodon passed the brachiosaur behind Tony, catching up to his rear. Mr. Slick continued firing at their vehicle, but wasn't able to swing his gun into June's window with the giant herbivore in the way.

June looked back up to the brachiosaur-driver. He didn't seem to notice the gunfire around him. Or, perhaps, he just didn't care.

Once both dinos were in front of the brachiosaurus, Tony slowed down.

"What the hell are you doing?" June asked.

"I've got a plan," Tony said.

Then the dimetrodon bit into the back of the stegosaur. June could hear the dimetrodon driver growling at the top of his lungs as his vehicle held the stegosaur's tail in its teeth.

"Was this part of your plan?" June asked.

"Hold on . . ." Tony said. He was beginning to look nervous.

Tony slowed down even more, so that all three vehicles on the road were bumper to bumper.

"Brace yourself," Tony said.

As the stegosaur began driving even slower, the gunfire stopped.

"Let go of its tail, you idiot!" Mr. Slick yelled down at the dimetrodon driver.

But Magic Steve couldn't hear Slick's whispery voice over the sound of his own roars. He was no longer a human. He was now a dinosaur. He had his prey between his teeth. He could taste its blood in his mouth. He would never let go.

"RRRAAAWR! RAAAAWR! RAAWR!"

As the brachiosaurus driver became impatient with the slow dinos in front of him, he attempted to jump two dinos at the same time.

"Let go of the tail!" Mr. Slick yelled.

When the brachiosaurs leapt into the air, Tony sped up, pulling the dimetrodon with him.

"Don't you dare!" June yelled at Tony. Then she screamed as she saw the brachiosaur's massive shadow coming down on them.

"RRRAAAWR! RAAAWR!"

As the stegosaurus flew forward, pulling the dimetrodon with it, Magic Steve could see a shadow growing larger and larger around his vehicle. When he realized it was a colossal dino coming down on him, he frowned and made a whimpering dinosaur sound.

"Rrreeewr?" Steve said.

Then his vehicle was crushed into the street, beneath the weight of the colossal brachiosaur.

"Holy shit," June said. She couldn't believe they made it out from under the massive dinosaur unscathed.

The dimetrodon was still trapped between the brachiosaur's legs. With every step of the colossal machine, the dimetrodon was mashed even further into a mangled heap, until the contorted pile of metal rolled out from under the brachiosaur onto the side of the road.

The brachiosaurus driver didn't pull over to check on the dimetrodon. He didn't even seem to notice what had happened.

June laughed as loud as she could. She didn't know exactly what she was laughing about. She just didn't know how else to react to what had just happened.

Tony bobbed his head with satisfaction. "That's what they

get for messing with Mr. Fast Awesome."

"Now what do we do?" June asked, a few more miles down Canyon Road.

"We should get off of the road," Tony said. "I think we should head south. Get a hotel. Lay low for a little while."

They passed a motel on the right.

"What about that one?" June asked.

"Not that one," Tony said. "We want to get as far away from this highway as possible. Once he sees the corpses we left back there, Rape Face is going to know we were headed east on Canyon."

June nodded. She trusted him.

"Besides," Tony said. "We don't want to stay at a roadside motel anyway. We need a hotel with a parking garage, so we can keep Santos hidden."

"Santos?" June asked.

"Oh, I never told you?" Tony smiled and patted the dashboard. "That's my stegosaur's name. Santos."

"Santos?" June said. Then she smirked.

She pet the dashboard with an armadillo shell.

"Thank you for rescuing me, Santos."

CHAPTER FIFTEEN

"There's only one bed," June said as they entered the hotel room.

"We'll have to make due, baby."

"You requested a king-size bed instead of two queens, didn't you?" June asked.

"It's just fate," he said.

Then he rolled a cart into the room with his stubby arms. There was a bottle of champagne in a bucket of ice with two wine flutes.

"There's no way in hell I'm ever going to sleep with you," June said. "Don't even try."

"The thought hadn't crossed my mind, Sugar Legs." He dimmed the lighting and lit two candles.

"Just because you helped me escape from those guys doesn't mean I owe you sex or anything," she said. "I'll pay you whatever money you want to help me through this. But sex isn't an option."

"Of course not, babydoll," Tony said, popping the champagne cork and filling the glasses with white foam. "I'm just trying to help you relax."

"Sure you are," June said, sitting down on the bed.

Tony crawled up on the bed behind her and began to massage her shoulders with his arm-stumps.

"You need to unwind after such a stressful experience," he said, rubbing her shoulders in little circles. "Let Mr. Fast Awesome take care of you."

Even though it creeped her out to have the amputee rubbing her with his arm-stumps, he was incredibly skilled at giving massages. She felt the tension slowly release from her muscles with each disturbing stroke.

"Do you like that?" Tony said over her shoulder.

"*Uh*," June said.

As he leaned his body against her for balance, June could feel a large bulge between Tony's amputated legs. He didn't have an erection, but even flaccid she could feel his penis on her back. She could tell the thing was huge. She tried to imagine exactly what size it must be when erect. In her head, she pictured it even larger than one of his leg stumps. She imagined him having difficulty walking around with a penis longer than his stubby legs.

Tony heard her giggling.

"That's right, baby," he said. "Enjoy yourself. For all we know, it could be our last night on Earth."

CHAPTER SIXTEEN

June dodged the concrete slab as it came down at her head. When it collided with Mr. Happy's corpse, his insides sprayed out in all directions like a frog under a sledgehammer.

The demonic executioner raised the club in the air again, his red eyes glaring at his prey through his spiked iron mask.

June got to her feet. The massive fire lining the warehouse walls blazed so high that the air burned her lungs when she tried to breathe. She looked over at Tony. He still wasn't moving. She wasn't going to leave him. She couldn't leave him. She had to defeat the crazed monster and get out of there as soon as possible.

"Let's go," June said to the hulk, returning to a boxing stance. "You don't scare me one bit."

She charged the muscular beast and punched him in the stomach. He didn't try to dodge. He just took it. The punch didn't faze him in the slightest. The armadillo coughed and writhed against his chest, as if her punch knocked the wind out of the creature.

"What the fuck are you?" June asked.

He just smacked her with his open palm, knocking her back. She regained her posture. Flaming chunks of wood fell from the ceiling all around her.

She noticed her armadillos were shaking. So were her knees. She wanted to just leave Tony and run away. Tony might be a dead man anyway. At least one of them would get out of there alive.

"I have to run away," June said to Tony. "How can I beat him?"

The hulk stomped slowly toward her. She stared at the large tattoo on the center of his chest. A tattoo of the number one.

"I couldn't even beat Mr. Sorry," she said. "How the hell am I going to beat this guy?"

She took a step back with every step the man took forward.

"It's hopeless," she said to herself.

CHAPTER SEVENTEEN

"Hopeless."

June stretched her fingers out and then clenched her fists until her knuckles turned white. She had no idea how she was going to go up against the champion, Tina Lee.

"There's no way," June said to herself. "I'm just going to make an idiot out of myself. She's so out of my league."

Her trainer said she would do just fine, but she knew he was blowing smoke up her ass. He knew she was going to lose no matter how hard she prepared. She could tell he figured this was the furthest she was ever going to go in her boxing career.

June let out all of her aggression on the punching bag. She felt safe fighting against the punching bag. It was an opponent she could always defeat.

Then she imagined the bag was Tina Lee's face. Her punches weakened. Even a vision of the champion was too intimidating to fight.

"I'm going to be demolished," June said.

She wished she had been taking steroids. Perhaps if she were stronger she'd be able to take on the champion. If only she was as tough as Muscle June, the boxer version of her from another dimension, the one with the armadillo fists.

June's eyes lit up. She remembered that Muscle June had offered to hook her up with the operation if she wanted.

"And you'd pay for it?" June had asked her doppelganger.

"Sure," said Muscle June. "You're me, aren't you? If you can't count on yourself for help, who can you count on?"

She decided to go through with it. That was the edge she needed. She didn't care if it turned her into a freak. With her new armadillo fists, June was going to pummel her opponent until she looked like roadkill under the foot of a ninety-ton brachiosaur.

CHAPTER EIGHTEEN

"What do you think could have done this?" Mr. Marathon asked, staring down at the wrecked dimetrodon.

"They were trampled," said Mr. Sorry.

Mr. Sorry kneeled down, examining the wreck.

"By what?" asked Mr. Marathon.

"A brachiosaurus," said Mr. Sorry.

"How do you know that?" asked Mr. Food, eating a candy bar.

"Because I know," said Mr. Sorry.

"Bullshit," said Mr. Food. "You're talking out your ass. There's no way you can tell by looking at this lump of metal."

Mr. Sorry didn't bother responding. He walked away from the fat guy, examining the other side of the dimetrodon corpse.

"Trust him," Mr. Happy told Food. "The guy used to be a detective."

"A detective?" Food said. "You've got to be shitting me."

"He used to be a cop on the boss' payroll," said Mr. Happy.

"They let that maniac be a cop?" asked Mr. Food.

"Yeah." Mr. Happy smiled. "He didn't last long as a cop. After he got out of jail for busting his partner's legs, the boss hired him on."

"No wonder why I hate the guy," said Mr. Food. "Pigs make me fucking sick."

"I can't find Mr. Slick's body anywhere," Mr. Marathon said to Rape Face.

"Did you check every piece of flesh scattered across this road, dick fingers?" Rape Face said.

"He's not here," said Mr. Marathon.

Rape Face scanned the area, squinting his tiny gray eyes. Then he pointed at a body in the nearby bushes.

"He's right there, dumbshit," said Rape Face.

Mr. Marathon went toward the body in the bushes. He leaned down and rolled the body over.

"It's not him," Mr. Marathon said.

"What?" Rape Face yelled, annoyed by the sound of the lanky man's voice.

"It's not Mr. Slick."

Rape Face spit tobacco juice. "Well, who the fuck is it then?"

Mr. Marathon shrugged. "I don't know. Some other guy."

CHAPTER NINETEEN

As the brachiosaurus came down on top of the dimetrodon, Mr. Slick jumped off of the roof. He hit the steel street and rolled off of the road. Looking back, he saw Magic Steve crushed beneath the feet of the enormous dinosaur.

He got to his feet and snapped his dislocated shoulder back into place. Once the brachiosaur finally kicked the crushed dimetrodon to the side of the road, Mr. Slick approached the wreckage. He knew Magic Steve was dead before he even saw the body. The annoying kid's flesh was pulverized within the metal wreck, as if he'd been through a garbage disposal.

Mr. Slick tried to reach into the wreck to get the phone, but he could only fit his hand ten inches within before hitting crumpled metal. Without any way to reach Mr. Face, Slick decided to continue the job on his own.

A guy riding a velociraptor came zooming by a few minutes later. Mr. Slick swung his yo-yo gun out in front of the man, the wire wrapping around the raptor rider's neck. When Slick yanked the yo-yo gun back, the rider flew off of the back of his dino and hit the ground with a broken neck.

"I need to borrow your ride," Mr. Slick whispered to the dead raptor rider.

After he pulled the body off of the road, Mr. Slick got onto the back of the velociraptor, revved its engine, and took off at full speed.

When Mr. Slick caught up to the stegosaurus, he didn't engage them. He knew Mr. Torso thought he was dead, so he was going to use that to his advantage. He wasn't going to attack until he had a better chance of success, once Mr. Torso was no longer behind the wheel of that stegosaurus.

He followed them east until they reached a small coastal city. When they arrived at a hotel, he parked across the street and watched them from a distance. He was going to stay back for a while, wait until they thought they were safe, then attack.

He wasn't going to rush in guns-blazing like usual. He was going to be patient. He was going to play it smart.

CHAPTER TWENTY

"Hey, Rape Face," Mr. Food said, stepping out of the triceratops.

Rape Face looked up from the dimetrodon wreckage and gave him a dirty look. "What did you just fucking call me?"

Food ignored his question. "I think I found Slick."

"Where?" asked Mr. Sorry.

"In Lily Port," Food said. "On the radio, they said some crazy guy was shooting up a hotel over there. The way they described him, especially his guns, it's got to be him."

"That fucking idiot," Rape Face said. "He went in guns-blazing as usual."

He climbed the ladder up the side of the T-rex.

"Why couldn't that asshole be patient?" Rape Face grumbled to himself. "He should've played it smart."

Then the five men got into their dinos and headed east, for Lily Port.

CHAPTER TWENTY-ONE

"Give me the room number of Tony Kudrow," Mr. Slick told the woman at the front desk of the hotel.

She could barely understand his soft voice. Then he whipped a gun out of his sleeve, pointed it at her, and repeated himself. She heard him the second time.

"I'll do anything you say," she told him, holding her hands up. "Just don't shoot. I've got kids at home."

"Everybody's got kids at home," said Mr. Slick. "Just hurry it up."

"Yeah, okay," she said. "Yeah."

After clicking through the records on her computer, she said, "Room 306."

"Give me the key," he said.

"Yeah, okay," she said. "Yeah."

She slid the key card across the desk.

"Thank you," Mr. Slick said, as he put the key card in his suit pocket.

Then he shot her in the face, just as three police officers entered the lobby.

CHAPTER TWENTY-TWO

Rape Face drove the T-rex down the road toward Lily Port, when a stegosaurus came racing past in the opposite direction.

"That was them," Mr. Sorry said.

Rape Face turned the T-rex around and followed. He hit the speaker phone and called the triceratops.

"They just passed us," Rape Face said.

"Yeah, we saw," said Mr. Food.

"Well then get the fuck after them, fat ass," Rape Face yelled.

When he slammed on the gas, the T-rex roared a metallic roar and then stomped down the road after the stegosaur.

CHAPTER TWENTY-THREE

June woke up in the hotel room. Police lights flashed through the sides of the curtains.

"What's wrong, baby?" Tony groaned, rubbing his hairy naked chest with his stumps. "Come back to bed."

When June looked out the window, she saw seven pentaceratops police cruisers in the parking lot.

"Something's going on," she said.

Tony stood up and pulled on his shorts. Then he raised his eyebrows at the sight of the boxer woman's bare ass and the sides of her breasts squished against the glass. But once he heard the gunshots, he snapped out of it.

"That Mr. Slick guy is still alive," June said.

"Huh?" Tony said, hobbling over to the window. "How?"

When Tony looked outside, he saw the cops shooting at somebody who was inside the hotel. Although he didn't see Mr. Slick himself, he saw the yo-yo guns as they extended into the parking lot to shoot down the cops hiding behind their vehicles.

"We need to get out of here," Tony said. "Fast."

CHAPTER TWENTY-FOUR

Mr. Slick was a yo-yo champion when he was younger, which was why he had become so skilled at his shooting technique. He used to perform yo-yo tricks at kid's birthday parties and at elementary schools. He did it just for fun in his early twenties. He had no idea the skills would come in handy once he was hired by Big Bob.

When the cops surrounded him in the hotel lobby, Mr. Slick spun his gun in a circle over his head, as if he were doing an around-the-world yo-yo trick. The cops fell to the ground with bullets in their heads.

One of them jumped over the front desk, so Mr. Slick did his walk-the-dog trick, rolling his yo-yo gun beneath the counter, filling the cop with holes.

He took the elevator up to the third floor. Some people had stepped out of their rooms, wondering what all the commotion was about. When they saw Mr. Slick coming toward them, they ducked back into their doorways. But that wasn't enough to escape him. Mr. Slick whirled his yo-yo guns down the hall, shooting them dead from their presumably safe positions.

CHAPTER TWENTY-FIVE

June opened the hotel room door and looked into the hallway. An obese man in boxer shorts stepped around the corner and fell to the floor, dead. His chest was covered in bullet holes.

"He's coming," June said.

Three police officers emerged from the stairwell behind her. As they passed her in the hallway, they said, "Get back in your room, ma'am."

They aimed their weapons at the end of the hallway, waiting for Mr. Slick to come around the corner. But instead of the assailant, a gun on a wire whirled out into their line of fire. The three policemen took bullets through their chests one at a time and hit the floor. Then Mr. Slick stepped around the hallway and faced June.

"Get back," June cried, leaping into the room toward Tony.

The yo-yo gun extended through their doorway and fired wildly into their room.

Mr. Slick ran down the hall toward room 306. When he got to the doorway, he saw Tony staring back at him on the other end of the room.

"Missed me, Mr. Small Dick," Tony said, and chuckled at his clever insult. "Don't you know that you have to aim lower if you want to hit me?"

Tony jumped behind the bed as Mr. Slick's yo-yo guns extended across the room, firing into the wall over Tony's back.

Before the guns returned to Slick's hands, June jumped out of the bathroom and caught his wires between her armadillos' teeth. Mr. Slick's eyes widened as the armadillos bit through the cables. His guns dropped limp on the other side of the room, behind the angry female boxer with armadillo fists. When her upper cut connected with his jaw, he was sent flying back into the hallway.

CHAPTER TWENTY-SIX

June's upper cut sent her opponent's jaw flying across the ring. The rest of his body still stood in front of her, but his lower jaw had been ripped off of his face on impact. The referee didn't stop the match, too busy laughing his ass off at the carnage.

The guy continued to box without his lower jaw, blood gushing down his neck, his tongue dangling in the air. He tried to block one of her punches to his face, but she hit so hard that her armadillo fist broke both of his forearms. He wasn't able to fight at all after that, just shriek in agony. Then her armadillo fist collided with his temple, sending bits of skull and brain into the air, across the mat.

June was a different person during this era in her life. She was Psycho June. After she was banned from professional boxing, she had no choice but to fight in the underground bare-knuckle tournaments. The audience was comprised of all manner of criminal scum, from crooked politicians, to drug lords, to Bobby "Big Bob" Mazetti.

When she entered these arenas, she was no longer the June who wanted to box because she thought it was fun. She came to do one thing: obliterate her opponent from the face of the planet. She was a warrior from hell with red demon eyes. Her armadillos would crush their skulls and feast on their blood.

After her opponent had fallen unconscious, June did not stop there. She jumped on top of his body, straddling his chest between her thighs, and continued to pound on his face long after the match was over. She punched until his skull shattered into chunky gore, and then she punched the chunks into a soupy puddle.

The referee never stopped her. The crowd never stopped her. She was their favorite. She was Psycho June Howard, aka Armadillo Fists. She gave them what they wanted, and what they wanted was to see a man's brains splattered across the ring as if a brontosaurus had run over his skull.

CHAPTER TWENTY-SEVEN

June promised herself she would never let Psycho June out ever again. She had murdered countless people in the ring when she allowed the demon to take over her spirit. That wasn't who she wanted to be anymore. That was in her past.

But when she climbed on top of Mr. Slick in the hallway of the hotel, she couldn't help but let the demon out a little. The bloodlust overwhelmed her.

She punched him in the face, with a left, then a right, alternating between armadillo fists. He gagged on his own blood and cried out between each punch. His pale white skin covered in pools of red, like strawberry syrup oozing down vanilla ice-cream.

Then June punched harder, harder, until his skull started cracking. She enjoyed the satisfying popping sound as her fist smashed his head open like a Halloween pumpkin. Her tongue licked at the blood as it splashed into her smiling face.

"June," Tony said, coming up behind her.

She giggled madly, punching the man's brains into mush.

"That's enough!" Tony said, smacking her back with his stump. "He's dead."

June snapped out of it and shook Psycho June out of her mind. When she looked at the gore coating the floor and walls around her, she began to cry.

"Come on," Tony said, pushing her away from the body. "We've got to get out of here."

June rose to her feet and wiped the tears away. Then she followed him to the stairwell.

Tony and June didn't notice the triceratops or the T-rex passing them as they drove down the highway on their way out of Lily Port.

"What was that back there?" Tony asked. His voice was softer than usual, concerned for her. "You seemed like a different person."

"I don't want to talk about it," June said.

Tony drove in silence for a while.

"You're dangerous, aren't you?" he asked.

June buried her face in her armadillos' bellies.

"I don't want to be," she said.

She promised herself, no matter what happened, she wouldn't let the demon out again.

CHAPTER TWENTY-EIGHT

She tried to hold back the demon inside of her as Mr. Sorry came toward her with black tears in his eyes. But she didn't know if she could beat him, even if she let the demon out. The second he had pulled her out of the stegosaurus by her hair, she knew she wasn't going to win this fight.

Every time she threw a punch, he dodged. No matter how fast her fists were, he was able to avoid them every single time, without fail. He didn't punch back, just stared at her with his calm soulless eyes, wiping away black tears as they rolled down his cheeks.

"How the hell are you so fast?" June said, barely able to catch her breath.

When he finally threw his first punch, she wasn't able to block in time. His fist curled up under her arms, into her stomach, beneath her ribcage. She crumbled and vomited into the dirt. She had never been hit so hard in her life. His fists were stronger than even her armadillos. They were like bricks. No, she thought, they were like miniature steel wrecking balls.

When she looked up at the stegosaurus, covered in bullet holes, she realized she didn't have a choice. She didn't know if Tony was even still alive in there. She had to do whatever it took to save him, even if it meant releasing the demon.

She stood up to Mr. Sorry and raised her fists. The blood-lust filled her eyes. She imagined smashing his skull into a pulpy mess. Her lips curled into a wicked smile.

As she aimed her fist at the center of his forehead, Mr. Sorry casually dodged her attack and punched her in the face. She was out cold before she hit the ground.

CHAPTER TWENTY-NINE

Bobby "Big Bob" Mazetti was a big fan of getting punched in the face. He paid June a large sum of money to come to his house every Thursday and beat the crap out of him with her armadillo fists.

"Hit harder," Big Bob told her. "Hit me until I puke."

The boss already had huge welts on his chest, a black eye, and blood coming out of his nose. He was sitting on a chair in his personal gym, his hand down his shorts, masturbating as June beat on him like a punching bag.

"Yeah, you like that?" June said.

Big Bob moaned.

"Uh!" she said, as she punched him in the face.

The boss liked when she said *uh!* every time she punched him. He liked her to talk in a sexy voice. She focused on the boss' face as she punched him, trying to ignore what he was doing in his pants. It was always like this. She was like some kind of cross between his boxing trainer and his personal dominatrix.

"Yeah, hit me harder," Big Bob said, masturbating furiously.

Rape Face barged into the room just before the old man was about to cum.

"Hey, Bob," Rape Face said.

"What the fuck do you want now?" the boss yelled. "Can't you see I'm busy here?"

"Slick's come for his money," Rape Face said.

"Are you fucking kidding me?" Bob said. "Just pay the guy. You're giving me blue balls over here."

"Pay him with what?"

"Christ almighty . . ." Bob banged the back of his head on the wall behind him. In the most condescending tone he could muster, he said, "By the front door, on the table, there's an envelope full of money with the words *Mister* and *Slick* written on it. You blind or just stupid?" He threw his shirt at Rape Face. "Next time use your brain before bothering me while I'm training."

The words bounced off of Rape Face. He was busy staring at June's sweaty legs. She wished she could get paid to punch that ugly asshole in the face for hours on end.

When Rape Face left, Big Bob said, "That guy's an idiot."

"Why do you call him Mr. Face?" June asked him.

"He was supposed to be the *face* of my organization," he said. "I wanted to be more of a behind the scenes guy. He was supposed to be the one managing everything. What a joke that turned out to be. The asshole can't take a shit without needing me to wipe his ass for him."

"Should we start over?" June asked.

Big Bob looked down at his crotch and frowned.

"Yeah," he said. "My cock ain't a rock anymore."

June didn't want to think about it, so she just punched him in the face until he shut up.

CHAPTER THIRTY

Tony pulled the stegosaurus over onto the side of the road and flipped the engine off.

"Why'd you stop?" June asked.

Tony looked over at her.

"We're not going another mile until you tell me what happened," he said.

June shrugged. "What do you mean?"

"Why'd you kill the boss?" he said. "I know the job you did for Big Bob was demeaning, but you couldn't have killed him just for that."

June looked away. She really didn't want to talk about it.

"I'm not sure I can continue to help you if you're not honest with me," he said. "To be frank, after what you did to Mr. Slick back there I'm beginning to get a little scared of you. The look in your eyes . . . you looked like some kind of psychotic freak."

"I'm not a psychotic freak!" she shrieked at him, in the voice of a psychotic freak.

Tony noticed she had an armadillo pointed at him. The little creature was growling and foaming at the mouth, staring at him with a thirst for blood. He slowly turned his head away from the armadillo and stared forward, keeping his hands on the controls, not making any sudden moves.

When June realized her threatening posture, she eased up and hid the armadillo between her thighs.

"I'm sorry," she said. "I don't want you to be scared of me."

Tony responded calmly, softly, "Then tell me what happened between you and Big Bob. I want to understand what you're going through."

June looked down at her armadillo fists.

"He pushed me into it," she said.

Then she told him the story.

CHAPTER THIRTY-ONE

"This ain't working," Big Bob said, struggling to get his penis erect.

June stopped punching him in the face.

"Let's try something new," Bob said.

He stood up and went over to the wrestling mat in the center of his gym. Then he raised his fists.

"I want to box," he said.

"You want to go a round with me, old man?" June said, smirking.

"Bare knuckle boxing," he said. "My fists versus your armadillos."

June was kind of worried. She'd always been the one doing the punching. She didn't like the idea of getting punched back. She was worried about letting out Psycho June.

"I'll pay you double," he said.

"You sure?" June said.

The old guy threw a punch and she blocked, then she punched him in the jaw.

"Yeah," said the old guy. "Harder."

She did a hook-jab combo and Big Bob moaned with pleasure. June could see a bulge rising in his shorts. She punched him again.

"*Hard* enough for you?" June said, feeling like a phone sex operator with a page full of cheesy lines meant to somehow be sexy.

Bob put one hand into his underwear and began to stroke himself. With the other, he punched at June. She dodged and hit him again. He didn't bother blocking.

"Time to get serious," Bob said.

He took off his shorts and underwear, tossing them over his shoulder.

June hopped from side to side, her fists raised to chin-level, staring at the naked old man in front of her. He'd never taken his pants off while masturbating in front of her before. It made her twice as uncomfortable.

His saggy bulbous flesh was covered in liver spots and long white hairs growing out of moles. His penis was fully erect and pointing at her. It was long and thin. It looked like a pencil covered in loose, rubbery, splotchy skin. His scrotum dangled halfway down his thighs and was dark gray in color, as if he'd been dragging it through the dirt for the past few days.

"Take your clothes off," Big Bob told her.

June paused. She stopped moving her feet, but didn't lower her fists.

"I'll pay you triple," he said.

"You said all I had to do was hit you," June said.

"That's all I want you to do," he said. "But I want you to do it with your clothes off."

"I don't think . . ."

"I'm not going to fuck you," he said. "I just want to box."

"In the nude?"

"It's going to be *wild*," Bob said, shaking his fists and penis at her.

"I don't think I can," she said.

"Then I'll pay you whatever the fuck you want," he yelled, curling his eyebrows at her. "You're starting to piss me off, damn it. Now take your fucking clothes off and let me punch those tight little titties of yours."

June was shaking as she took her clothes off. The amount of money Big Bob was offering her was too much to refuse. And the angry look in his eyes told her that if she were to refuse him one more time he was going to put a bullet in her lungs.

She faced him on the wrestling mat and held up her armadillo fists.

"Let's go," he said, raising his fists to meet hers.

She threw a weak punch and he dodged it. Then he punched

her with all of his strength, right in the eye. She fell to one knee.

"Fight for real," Bob yelled at her, his erection becoming soft. "Don't fuck with me."

When she got back to her feet, he punched her in the stomach and then in the nose.

"You think I'm fucking around?" he said.

Blood dribbled from her nostrils.

She curled her armadillos and went at him, punching him in the stomach, and then the face. His penis was getting hard again. He threw a punch and she dodged, and then she kneed him in the stomach. He bowed over and stepped back.

"That was an illegal move," he said, chuckling. "But I'll let it slide. I kind of liked it."

Then she fought him like a real opponent, as if she was back in the ring again.

"Yeah," he said, blood spraying from his lips. "More."

She clocked him in the side of the head, then jabbed him in the center of the chest. He was jerking himself off as she threw the next punch.

"Harder," he said.

She punched him again. She couldn't punch him with all of her strength, worried about letting the demon out, worried what might happen to him.

"It's not hard enough!" he said, hitting her in the left nipple.

She backed away. He came at her, aiming only at her breasts. The creepy feeling of his old man knuckles touching her bare breasts was even worse than the pain they delivered.

"Come on," he said. "I know you've got more power than this. I've seen it."

He stopped punching her breasts and grabbed at them instead. She tried punching him in the face, and he dodged, grabbed her by the nipple and squeezed.

As he twisted her pink nugget of flesh, June clenched her teeth, pulled back her arm, and then threw all her weight into a punch to his face.

She heard a loud crack as her armadillo fist connected with

his forehead. He ejaculated onto her thighs and then fell back onto the mat, out cold.

June pulled her clothes back on, glancing over at her boss, wondering when he was going to stand back up. She was happy it didn't escalate any further. She was happy that the demon didn't come out. Had the bloodlust taken over, she would have beat the man to death and his skull would be in tiny bloody pieces all over the room. Then her life would be over. If his men didn't kill her, the cops would have put her in prison for the rest of her life.

She wiped her sweat on a towel and then held it to her nostrils tightly to stop the nosebleed. When she looked back at the old man, he didn't seem to be moving at all.

"You alright?" she asked him.

He didn't seem to be breathing.

"You okay?"

She went over to him and placed Jocko onto his shoulder. He didn't react when she shook him. She put the armadillo to his neck, but couldn't feel a pulse.

"Oh, shit," she said.

She shook him furiously.

"Come on, Bob. You can't be dead, you old bastard."

But no matter what she did, he wouldn't wake up. The demon didn't come out of her, but she had killed him anyway. She looked around. She wasn't sure what she should do. So she decided to get the hell out of there.

After she grabbed her stuff, she ran for the door, only to run into Rape Face as he entered the room with a question for the boss.

"What the fuck's going on here?" Rape Face asked.

June panicked. She punched the creep right in his rapey face, knocking him to the ground. Then she took off, down the hallway, toward the exit.

CHAPTER THIRTY-TWO

Rape Face rubbed his jaw as he drove the T-rex down the highway. It was still sore from when the boxer bitch punched him in the face.

He hit the speaker phone on the dashboard.

"Pull over at the gas station up ahead here," he said to the men in the triceratops.

"Why're we stopping?" Mr. Sorry asked.

"We're splitting up," Rape Face said. "I want you to go with the other guys in the triceratops and keep following Torso. I've got some business to take care of."

"What kind of business?" Mr. Sorry asked.

Rape Face spit tobacco juice as he pulled the T-rex into the gas station. "The kind of business that's none of your fucking business."

Mr. Sorry adjusted his glasses. "Very well."

Rape Face said, "Shoot the bitch on sight. I want her dead by sunrise, you got me? Use Mr. Corpse if you have to."

"You sure you want to use Mr. Corpse?" Sorry asked.

"Do whatever it takes to kill the broad and the halfy," said Rape Face. "Don't fuck me on this." He straightened his teeth in the rearview mirror. "I'll catch up with you guys later."

Mr. Sorry opened the dino door and stepped out onto the ladder attached to the side of the T-rex's torso.

"Dead on sight," Rape Face repeated.

"It'll be done by morning, boss," Mr. Sorry said, descending the ladder to the parking lot below.

Rape Face smiled proudly when he heard the word *boss*. He figured it was about time the boys started showing him a little respect.

CHAPTER THIRTY-THREE

Mr. Sorry preferred riding with Mr. Happy and Mr. Food in the triceratops, anyway. The three of them would make a good team for taking care of Mr. Torso and Armadillo Fists. It wasn't very long at all before they caught up to their targets.

"There they are," Mr. Sorry said, pointing at a stegosaurus up ahead.

It was pulled over on the side of the road. He could tell the woman and the amputee were in there, wrapped up in conversation.

"This is our chance," Mr. Sorry said. "Get ready to fire. They won't even see us coming."

Mr. Food and Mr. Sorry raised their machine guns to the windows. Mr. Happy stayed focused on the road.

"Aim for the driver," Sorry told Food.

Food grunted. There was a giant gas station pickle in his mouth.

As Mr. Happy slowed down, they opened fire on the stegosaurus. The bullets shredded the metal body, starting at its tail, through the driver's side door, and then all the way to its head.

Before the triceratops could turn around, Mr. Sorry leapt out of the window. Mr. Food and Mr. Happy looked at him with alarm as their boss' lieutenant jumped from the moving vehicle with reckless abandon.

Mr. Sorry rolled onto his feet and stood upright. Then he aimed his machine gun at the front of the stegosaurus and stepped forward. He didn't hear the police sirens coming down the street toward him.

CHAPTER THIRTY-FOUR

After June finished telling him the story, Tony asked, "So that's how it happened? That's how you killed the boss?"

June nodded her head. She had tears in her eyes.

Tony felt bad forcing her to retell the experience. He was happy that he could trust her again, but he understood why she didn't want to get into the details.

"If you ask me," Tony said, "that fucker got what he deserved."

June smiled at him for saying that.

"I know," June said, wiping her tears away.

He smiled back at her.

"I promise you, Sugar Legs," Tony said, rubbing her thigh with a stump-arm. "I'm going to get you through this. No matter what happens, I'll never leave your side."

Then he winked at her.

She leaned in to give him a kiss, but stopped short. Something caught her attention in the corner of her eye. But it was too late to do anything about it.

Gunfire erupted outside of the dino as the triceratops drove by. Mr. Sorry and Mr. Food sprayed the stegosaurus with bullets, all the way across the driver's side of the vehicle. June covered her head as glass, fluids, and bits of steel scattered around her like confetti.

When the gunfire stopped, Tony looked down at his stomach. There were holes in his orange spandex shirt. Blood oozed out of his torso, onto the seat.

"No," June cried, catching him as he toppled over.

His eyes were rolling in his head. She didn't know what to do. She wrapped him in her arms, rubbing his forehead, kissing him on the top of his head.

"Come on," she cried. "Tony! Mr. Awesome!"

He wasn't responding to her. She tried to put pressure on

his stomach wounds, but with the shape of her hands it didn't seem to do any good. Her armadillos just snuggled against his belly, licking at his blood.

When she looked up through the windshield, Mr. Sorry was standing in front of the vehicle, staring at her. He casually walked up the head of the stegosaurus, pointing his machine gun at them. Then he opened fire.

CHAPTER THIRTY-FIVE

Mr. Sorry stood on the roof of the stegosaurus, firing down into the vehicle. He knew the boxer girl was hiding somewhere in the backseat, but wasn't sure exactly where. So he fired multiple shots into the roof with each step he took.

The police sirens had scared away his partners. The triceratops never turned around to assist him. They kept on going, leaving him to deal with both the boxer and the cops.

Just as the police pentaceratops pulled up behind the stegosaurus, Mr. Sorry's gun clicked empty.

"Drop the weapon!" the cops yelled, jumping out of their dino and aiming their guns at him.

He tossed his machine gun aside.

"Raise your hands and step slowly off of the vehicle," one cop yelled, as the two policemen inched their way toward him.

He walked slowly down the stegosaurus tail and dropped down to the dirt, but he didn't raise his hands.

"I said raise your hands!"

Mr. Sorry paused. He raised one hand, adjusted his glasses, and lowered it again. Then, casually, he walked toward them. They opened fire.

CHAPTER THIRTY-SIX

June watched from the back seat of the stegosaurus as Mr. Sorry approached the cops. She couldn't believe her eyes. The cops were firing at the man in black, but all of their bullets were missing him, as if they were passing through a ghost's body.

Staring more carefully, June figured out what was happening. As implausible as it seemed, Mr. Sorry was dodging their bullets. His movement nearly imperceptible as he subtly weaved his way through the barrage.

Then, in the blink of an eye, Mr. Sorry flew forward fifteen feet and planted his fists into each of their chests. The cops froze, their guns still pointed at his previous position. Then their weapons tumbled from their fingers and they fell over, dead. His punches had stopped their hearts.

He turned to the stegosaurus and casually walked back toward June. He removed his leather gloves, revealing a number three tattooed on the back of his right hand.

June crawled into the front seat and started the engine, trying to pull Tony away from the controls. He was still alive, but just barely. She looked back. Mr. Sorry was moving slowly toward the back of the vehicle.

When she looked forward again, Mr. Sorry was already at the driver's side window, able to move a dinosaur's length faster than she could turn her head. He grabbed her by the hair and pulled her out of the window.

CHAPTER THIRTY-SEVEN

June awoke to one of her armadillo hands licking her face. She blinked twice, but couldn't see a thing. Everything was pitch-black. She tried to get up and banged her head against a very low ceiling, like she was inside of a coffin, buried alive.

A loud ringing was in her ears, so she also couldn't hear anything. Feeling around the edges of her tomb, she realized it wasn't a coffin at all. She was inside of a trunk. She guessed it was the trunk of the triceratops. Mr. Sorry was taking her back to Rape Face for execution.

"So this is how it ends," June said to the black, but couldn't hear her own words through the ringing in her ears.

She rolled over into a squatting position and readied her right fist. She might die soon, but the second Rape Face opened the trunk he was going to get one last clock to the jaw.

While sitting in the dark, waiting for the trunk lid to open for what seemed like an eternity, she cursed the day she met Big Bob. If only he had never come into her life none of this would have ever happened.

CHAPTER THIRTY-EIGHT

"You were amazing out there tonight," Big Bob said to June as he entered the locker room. "But then, you're always amazing. I've been to all of your matches."

June didn't look at him, busy washing blood and chunks of brain from her armadillos' shells.

"I don't sign autographs," she said.

Big Bob cough-laughed at her words.

"I didn't actually come for your autograph," he said. "But I guess you could say I'm a fan."

June dried Jocko off with a towel, while Judy attacked his tail.

"Well, sorry to break the news to you," June said, "but that was my last match. I've just decided to retire."

"Quit?" Big Bob said. "But you're the best. How can you quit?"

"Personal reasons," she said.

Big Bob rubbed his bristly chin.

"So what are you going to do now?" he asked. "For money?"

"I don't know," she said. "Maybe become a new attraction at a carnival freak show."

He snickered. She wasn't really joking.

"Why don't you come work for me?" he asked.

June looked up at him. She knew who he was. She knew what kind of work he was offering her. But doing the dirty work for some crime boss wasn't the kind of new life she was looking for.

"I recently lost my number four," said Big Bob. "If I hired you on, I think you would fit that rank just perfectly. That is, as long as you're willing to tattoo a number four somewhere on your body."

June wasn't listening anymore. She didn't want to have anything to do with him.

"I'm not interested in that kind of work," June said. "If you would have asked me a couple months ago I would have jumped at the offer. But not now. I'm done with violence."

Big Bob stared at her as she bandaged up her armadillos. Every once in a while their shells would get torn against an opponent's tooth or a jagged piece of skull bone. She had to take good care of their injuries. As Bob watched her, his eyes lit up.

"I've got another idea," he said. "This job won't be violent. It would be more like training, I guess you could say. I'll pay you twice what you were getting for your matches here. You'd come over once a week, for an hour's worth of work."

"You want me to be your personal trainer or something?" she asked.

"Yeah, something like that," he said.

She agreed to give it a try, even though he hadn't given her all of the details. She would be making a hell of a lot more she made in the underground boxing matches and she wouldn't have to let the demon out anymore. For just an hour's worth of work per week she was willing to put up with anything. No matter what Big Bob had in mind.

"I'll have one of my drivers pick you up next Thursday, around six," he said.

CHAPTER THIRTY-NINE

Outside the abandoned factory, Mr. Happy sat on top of the triceratops, lighting a corncob pipe filled with cinnamon tobacco.

"That cinnamon shit smells good, man," Mr. Food said, throwing rocks across the yard. "It's giving me a craving for some fucking snickerdoodles."

Mr. Happy chuckled. "You like snickerdoodles?"

"I fucking love snickerdoodles," said Mr. Food, throwing another rock. "You got a problem with that?"

Mr. Food was aiming his stones at an old rusted out pliosaur. By the look of it, the ocean craft probably hadn't been seaworthy for decades.

"I'm bored," said Food Mountain. "I want to get some dinner and some pussy. When are we going to be done with this shit? It's almost morning."

"It probably won't be much longer," said Mr. Happy. "Mr. Face should be here soon."

Food Mountain tossed his last rock and groaned loudly. Then he went to the triceratops, took the key out of the ignition, and went toward the ass of the dino.

Mr. Happy sat upright, smiling, "What are you doing?"

"I need something to pass the time," said the fat man, putting the key into the trunk. "I'm going to take out my frustration on this bitch's tight little twat while she's still unconscious."

He put the key into the trunk.

"Mr. Sorry said to leave her in there until he got back," said Mr. Happy.

"Fuck Mr. Sorry," said Food Mountain. "He can suck my fat dick."

As he opened the trunk, an armadillo flew at him, punched him in the face, and knocked him on his ass.

CHAPTER FORTY

Tony tried to stay motionless as his ex-coworkers hovered over him outside of the stegosaurus.

"Is he dead?" Mr. Happy asked.

"Are you kidding me?" said Food Mountain. "Look at how many holes we put in him."

Tony could hear the sound of someone chewing on a giant gas station pickle near the driver's side window. After the sound of their footsteps wandered away from his position, Tony peeked up over the dashboard, trying to block the agony of the bullets in his guts.

He saw Mr. Happy and Mr. Food place June in the back of the triceratops, as Mr. Sorry waited in the cab for them. When they drove away, Tony counted to twenty and then started his stegosaurus, got on the road and followed after them.

As he drove, he took the cigarette lighter from the dashboard and jammed it inside of the bullet holes in his belly, one at a time. It took several tries with each wound before the arteries were completely cauterized and the bleeding stopped. He didn't know how long he was going to last with the metal slugs in his guts, but as long as he wasn't bleeding to death there was still time to save June.

CHAPTER FORTY-ONE

After she clobbered the fat guy, June leapt out of the trunk of the triceratops and took off running. Mr. Food wobbled to his feet and chased after her.

"You're going to be sorry if you let her get away," Mr. Happy yelled from the roof of the mechanical dinosaur.

"She's not going anywhere," Mr. Food yelled, barreling after the girl like a stampeding elephant.

June couldn't believe how fast he was for such a fat guy. Although all of the rolls of fat bounced up and down as he ran, his legs moved like they were made of pure muscle. He quickly caught up to her and tackled her to the ground.

As she struggled to get out of Mr. Food's arms, June felt his sausagey fingers squirming to get between her thighs.

"Come on, bitch," he said. "Let me have that pussy of yours while your heart's still beating."

She shrieked at the thought of being sexually assaulted by the morbidly obese gangster. As he pulled at her boxing shorts, she punched him in the face, loosening his grip. Then she crawled out from under him.

June realized she wasn't going to be able to run away from this abnormally fast fat guy, so she had no choice but to fight him. She raised her fists and got into a boxing stance. Her feet danced in the dirt around him.

"You wanna go, bitch?" asked Mr. Food, getting to his feet. "Okay, let's go."

He unbuttoned his shirt.

"I don't care if you've got those ugly critters on your hands," he said. "They might as well be pillows."

He pulled off his shirt, revealing hairy rolls of lard. When he turned to face June, she saw the number ten was tattooed on his chest.

"You're only number ten?" June asked, smirking.

"Yeah, I'm number ten," he said, smiling and raising his fists to his chin. "So what?"

"You know I pummeled number five to death, right?" she said.

The smile slid from Food Mountain's face. "You killed Slick?"

She nodded and held up her armadillos. "With my bare fists."

Food shivered for a second, but just a second. Then he shook it off.

"Fuck Slick," he said. "He's useless without his guns. I could have taken him myself if we went fist to fist."

June shrugged. "If your brains end up scattered across the yard, don't say I didn't warn you."

June's punches had no effect on him. The guy's fat was like rubber. She leaned over, trying to catch her breath.

"I told you," Food said. "Your armadillos might as well be pillows. I don't feel a thing under these layers of meat."

He waved his belly at her like a flag.

"Fat piece of shit," she said.

Mr. Food just laughed.

"Call me what you will, tiny tits," he said. "But eventually you're going to wear yourself down. Then, once you're too weak to stand, I'm going to stick my dick inside you and fill your hole with my thick, creamy man-sauce."

"Eww," she said, gagging at the word *man-sauce*. "You even try sticking your dick anywhere near me and you're going to lose it."

"I'm going to lose it all over your face," he said.

June charged him and punched rapidly into his belly with both fists, treating the tub of fat like a punching bag. He just stared down and laughed at her, not feeling a thing as she went to town. Then he wrapped his arms around her, picked her up off the ground, and licked her neck. She cringed as his thick tongue slimed down her chest toward her cleavage.

"Let me taste you," said the fat man.

She shoved her fist into his face, but instead of punching him she opened the armadillo and let Jocko bite into his tongue. Mr. Food screamed and let go of her. He backed away, holding his mouth.

"You fucking bitch," he said. "My tongue means everything to me."

June regained her composure and glared at Food.

"Okay, fat man," she said. "Time to get serious."

She raised her fists out to her sides. Then she slowly opened them, uncurling the armadillos.

"What are you going to do?" Mr. Food said, backing away.

She charged at him with open hands, the armadillos' mouths snarling and gnashing their teeth. Mr. Food squealed as the armadillos attacked him. They clawed and bit at his man-breasts and fat rolls, growling like rabid rodents.

"Get them away from me," he yelled. "Get them away!"

Then she slammed both of her hands against the sides of his head. The armadillos hooked their claws into his face, digging deep into the flesh.

"You fucking bitch," he said, whimpering.

She glared at him, her armadillos' claws sinking deeper into his skin.

"Stop," he yelled at her.

She smiled, digging her claws even deeper. That's when she noticed she was letting the demon out. She shook her head, trying to fight it.

"Stop what you're doing," he yelled.

But the sensation of his flesh between her claws made the demon thirsty. It wanted blood. Then she shook her head, repeating to herself *I can't let the demon out.*

"I can't let the demon out," said Mr. Food.

When the fat guy said this, June cocked her head. It was as if he were reading her mind. As the fire burned in her eyes, she could feel it. She could feel the demon coming out of her.

"The demon's coming," said Mr. Food.

Psycho June smiled at the fat man. "You're damn right it is."
Then her armadillos ripped his face off.

Psycho June backed away, with one side of Mr. Food's face dangling from Jocko's mouth. The other side dangled from Judy's. But Mr. Food didn't scream. He glared at her with blood red eyes. June breathed deeply and the demon sank to the back of her mind. She dropped the pieces of face onto the ground.

"You shouldn't have done that," said a voice behind her shoulder.

She turned to see Mr. Happy a few yards back, smiling and smoking his tobacco pipe.

"Done what?" June asked him.

He raised his pipe and pointed over at Mr. Food. The faceless morbidly obese man was angry, growling. He reached up and ripped the rest of his face off. Then he grabbed his manbreasts and tore them off of his body. June's mouth dropped open as she watched the fat man rip chunks of blubber from his body and throw them on the ground.

"What the hell is going on?" June said to the man in the yellow suit.

The fat man wasn't really fat. All of the lard was fake, prosthetic. Once all of the fat was removed from Mr. Food's body, another man stood before them, a man of pure muscle. June noticed that the number ten was no longer tattooed on this man's chest. The zero had been ripped away with the prosthetic lard. The tattoo was now a number one.

"You've awakened Mr. Corpse," said the man in the yellow suit.

June backed away. "Who the hell is Mr. Corpse?"

Mr. Happy took a puff on his tobacco pipe.

"The man standing before you is not just one person. He is two people. He has split personalities. And they each have a different role in Big Bob's organization."

The massive man bent down and stuck his hand inside of the piles of lard. Then he pulled out a spiked iron mask. He placed it over his face obscuring every feature but his red blazing eyes.

"He is ranked both number ten *and* number one," Mr. Happy said, smiling. "You might have been able to defeat Mr. Food, but it won't be so easy to beat Mr. Corpse. He's the most deranged evil killing machine ever to be born."

June shook her head.

"I can't fucking believe this shit," she said, as the beast stomped toward her.

CHAPTER FORTY-TWO

When the triceratops arrived at the abandoned warehouse, Mr. Sorry wasn't sure what he was going to do with Armadillo Fists. He sat with Mr. Happy and Mr. Food for a while, waiting for Rape Face to show up. Then he decided to go for a walk.

"Wait here," he told them, adjusting his glasses. "I'm going to have a look around the place."

"Whatever you say," Mr. Happy said, sitting on the roof of the triceratops, smiling and packing a bowl of tobacco in his corncob pipe.

"Leave the girl in the trunk," Sorry told them. "Don't do anything until I get back."

Mr. Food threw a rock across the yard. "Weren't we supposed to kill the broad before Rape Face got here?"

"We'll get to that later," said Mr. Sorry.

"I can kill her while you're gone if you want," said Mr. Food. "I've got nothing better to do."

"Just leave her in the trunk," said Mr. Sorry. "Don't kill her until I say it's time to kill her."

Mr. Food shrugged and threw another rock.

As Mr. Sorry strolled around the property, trying to organize some thoughts in his head, he saw a tyrannosaurus rex parked on the other side of the building. It was Rape Face's T-rex. He was already there, but he was nowhere in sight.

Mr. Sorry wandered through the warehouse, looking for the old man. He wasn't inside so he went out back, scanning the landscape. There was movement at the top of a nearby hill. He squinted until he made out the shape of a man. It was Rape Face.

"What the hell are you doing up there, Rapey?"

There was a shovel in Mr. Face's hands. He was digging a hole. It looked like he'd been at it for a while. Mr. Sorry wiped a tear from his eye and hiked up the hill toward him, to see what the heck was going on.

CHAPTER FORTY-THREE

June ran at Mr. Corpse and punched him in the stomach. His abs were rock solid. He didn't feel a thing. He glared down at her and slapped her on the chest. It sent her flying across the yard outside of the abandoned warehouse. She landed shoulder-first in the dirt. Mr. Happy smiled down at her as she rolled over near his feet.

"It doesn't look like you're making any progress," Mr. Happy said. "Perhaps you should get back into the trunk."

June got to her feet and clenched her fists.

"No thanks," she said.

She didn't have a choice. She was going to have to release Psycho June. It was the only way she could possibly stand a chance.

The bloodthirsty hulk stomped toward her, but she didn't back away. She let the demon inside of her rise to the surface. She let Psycho June out to play.

Psycho June smiled with hungry eyes. She was not intimidated by this hulk. Such a challenge only excited her more. Raising her fists sideways like batwings, she charged forward. Then a mechanical stegosaurus barreled into the yard and trampled Mr. Corpse into the dirt.

CHAPTER FORTY-FOUR

Tony was in his stegosaurus, watching the warehouse from a distance, waiting for his chance to come in and rescue June. He didn't want to rush in too quickly. He knew he'd only have one chance and didn't want to blow it.

He saw Mr. Corpse punch June in the chest. It sent her flying across the yard of the abandoned warehouse, into the dirt. He knew he couldn't wait any longer. This had to be his time to act. He had to go in and help her. Otherwise, she would be obliterated.

Tony had heard stories about Mr. Corpse, but didn't know that he was Mr. Food's alter ego. He knew Mr. Corpse was a bloodthirsty animal, who had only one desire and that was to kill everything in his path. Some of the lesser ranked men in Big Bob's organization used to tell ghost stories about how Mr. Corpse was some kind of deformed psychopath that Big Bob kept locked in his basement, feeding him the flesh of his enemies. Tony had assumed he was only a myth.

As he pulled his stegosaurus out from behind a wall of trees, he saw June throwing fists at the masked demon, not a single one having any effect. He slammed his leg-stump on the gas and roared toward the warehouse, toward Mr. Corpse.

The stegosaurus trampled over the muscled monstrosity as Tony plowed through the yard.

"What the fuck!" Psycho June yelled, as if angry at Mr. Torso for cheating her out of her fight.

But when she saw the stegosaurus crash into the side of the warehouse, the demon faded from her mind.

"Tony!" she yelled, running for the dino. She was amazed

he was still alive.

Before she could get to him, Mr. Corpse sat up and pulled himself to his feet. He wasn't dead yet. Standing between her and the stegosaurus, the demonic executioner couldn't be avoided. June had to go through him.

She charged the monstrous man and hit him with both fists at once. Not in his face or body, but in his thighs. This knocked him off balance and he stumbled backward. Then Tony swung the stegosaurus' tail at him. The spikes impaled his chest and threw him to the ground. Then his arms went limp. His eyes went blank.

As June looked down at Mr. Corpse, she felt a little sorry for him. She could relate to what the man was going through. Of course, what was going on in June's mind was different. Mr. Corpse and Mr. Food were this person's split personalities, but June didn't have split personalities. The demon inside of her was not somebody else living inside of her. *She* was Psycho June. It wasn't another identity. It was a normal part of her personality that she had to suppress.

CHAPTER FORTY-FIVE

Mr. Sorry climbed the hill behind the warehouse toward Rape Face.

"You got here early," he said to Mr. Face.

The old man jumped at the sound of Mr. Sorry's voice and turned around. He had a shovel in his hand and there was a freshly dug hole at his feet. Inside the hole lay a dead man. It was Mr. Marathon.

"What happened to him?" Mr. Sorry asked.

Rape Face looked down at the corpse and shrugged.

"What's it fucking matter?" Rape Face said. "The guy was an asshole."

Then he shoveled dirt over the corpse. There were two bullet holes in his chest.

"You killed him?" Mr. Sorry asked.

Rape Face ignored the question. Instead, he asked, "You got the boxer bitch?"

"In the trunk," said Mr. Sorry.

"Why isn't she dead yet?"

Mr. Sorry didn't respond. He picked up an extra shovel from the dirt and helped him dig a second hole.

"We need to make sure we kill the bitch's armadillos after we shoot her," Rape Face said. "Those things are burrowing animals. We don't want them digging her body out after we bury her."

CHAPTER FORTY-SIX

After Mr. Corpse's body went limp, metal spikes jutting out of his chest, Tony said, "I told you, Sugar Legs . . ." Then he raised an arm-stump out of the stegosaurus window with what little strength he had left. "I told you I would never leave your side."

June ran toward the stegosaurus, but stopped in her tracks as a pool of fire erupted between them. She turned around to see Mr. Happy standing there with a big smile on his face.

"I guess it's up to me to take care of you now," Mr. Happy told them.

He opened his yellow suit to reveal a dozen Molotov cocktails lining the inside of his coat. He pulled one of them out, lit it with his tobacco pipe as he puffed on the mouthpiece, and then tossed it at the stegosaurus.

Tony crawled out of the dino's window and landed on his stumps, as the Molotov exploded against the stegosaurus' bony back plates. Mr. Happy threw another one. It went through the shattered back window of the mechanical dinosaur. Before Tony could hobble away from the vehicle, before June could reach him, the stegosaurus exploded. It sent the human torso into the air and through a warehouse window.

June turned back and glared at Mr. Happy with tears in her eyes. Then she ran through the flames, charging into the warehouse, after Tony.

"That should be so, so sad," Mr. Happy said, pulling out another Molotov cocktail. "But it only makes me happy. So very, very happy."

As Mr. Happy entered the warehouse, he saw June trying to wake Mr. Torso. He was either dead or unconscious, but it didn't seem to matter either way to Mr. Happy. He lit another Molotov cocktail and tossed it at them. June rolled across the floor with Tony in her arms, dodging the pool of flames as it erupted from the broken bottle.

"I'm sorry for being so cruel," said Mr. Happy. "But I have no other choice."

He threw a beer bottle of gasoline at them. June dodged and it exploded into a sheet of fire along the wall behind her.

"Do you know why they call me Mr. Happy?" he asked June.

She didn't respond, pulling Tony into the center of the room, trying to get him away from the fire growing around them.

Mr. Happy continued, "I'm called Mr. Happy because I'm always happy. I can't stop being happy. I'm intensely, consistently, unreasonably happy . . . every waking second of every day."

Once she felt Tony was in a safe spot, June stood up and raised her fists to Mr. Happy.

"The doctors say it's a neurological condition," said Mr. Happy. "Something in my brain just keeps me in a good mood no matter what happens. My wife leaves me, I am happy. My uncle is murdered in his own home, I am happy."

He tossed a Molotov at June. The bottle bounced off an armadillo punch and flew over her head, exploding against a stack of wood.

"Do you know what it's like to be constantly happy *all* the time?" he said. Then he puffed on his tobacco pipe to light another cocktail. "It's absolutely maddening."

June dodged the next cocktail. She had to figure out a way to get to him, without setting herself on fire.

"No other emotions can ever get through," he said. "I never feel sadness, or anger, or fear. Only happiness. And without those emotions, I can't even enjoy being happy."

June charged toward him before he could light another cocktail. But Mr. Happy pulled an unlit one from his coat and held it up, as if to throw it at her. She froze. She knew she wouldn't make it out of there alive if covered in gasoline.

"That's why I got a job working for my crooked uncle, God bless his soul," he said. "I wasn't a bad guy before I had this disorder. I was just a normal nice guy with a normal life. But one day I woke up happy for no logical reason. I only became happier and happier with each passsing day. It never stopped. The reason I wanted to work for my dear uncle was so that I could do horrible, horrible things to people. I hoped that by doing horrible things I would feel something other than happiness. Guilt, pity, disgust, sadness—*any* emotion would do as long as it would stop me from being happy for even a fraction of a second."

He lit a Molotov and tossed it between them, so that she couldn't get at him without crossing the pool of fire. He paced along the flames.

"That's why I like to burn people," he said. "It's a horrible, brutal way to kill a person. When I see someone covered in liquid fire, dying an agonizing death, it's the closest I ever come to ruining my good mood."

He raised his last Molotov and aimed it at Tony.

"Especially when that person has a loved one nearby to watch them burn," he said, smiling widely.

CHAPTER FORTY-SEVEN

Mr. Sorry and Rape Face finished digging the second hole. As Sorry wiped the sweat from his brow, he noticed the warehouse was on fire.

"I wonder what's happening over there," said Mr. Sorry.

When he turned to Rape Face, he saw a gun pointed at him.

"It looks like we're going to need to dig a third hole," said Rape Face. "One about your size."

Mr. Sorry stared at him, black tears dripping down his cheeks.

"I think there's already enough holes," said Mr. Sorry.

The man in black approached the old man. Rape Face fired. Mr. Sorry's head cocked to the side and the bullet whizzed past his ear.

"You'll fit just nicely into the one we just dug," said Mr. Sorry, as he continued walking forward.

Rape Face fired three more shots. Even though he was only six feet away, Mr. Sorry dodged the slugs like gnats flying around his head. The bullets flew past him, toward the warehouse.

CHAPTER FORTY-EIGHT

As Mr. Happy tossed the Molotov at Tony's unconscious body, a bullet burst through a warehouse window and hit him between the eyes. The Molotov went over Tony's head, exploding against the wall behind him. Mr. Happy was still smiling as his corpse hit the floor.

The fire blazed around them. June looked down at Tony. She had to get him out of there.

As she dragged him inch by inch across the warehouse floor, she said, "You're heavy for a man with no arms or legs."

CHAPTER FORTY-NINE

"Stand still, you fucker," Rape Face said, as Mr. Sorry dodged his bullets.

No matter how close Mr. Sorry came to him, no matter where he aimed, Rape Face couldn't hit him. The man in black dodged calmly, effortlessly, as the bullets flew past him. When he was down to his last bullet, Rape Face stepped forward and pressed the barrel of the gun to Mr. Sorry's nose.

"Dodge this, you prick," said Rape Face.

Mr. Sorry stared past the gun, looking deep into the old man's eyes. A black tear rolled down his cheek, across the barrel of the gun, and down Rape Face's fingers.

The gun fired and the bullet burst through the top of Rape Face's head.

Within the split second between the old man pulling the trigger and the bullet leaving the chamber, Mr. Sorry grabbed Rape Face's wrist and twisted it around so the barrel was pointed up under his chin. The bullet traveled through his ugly, rapey face, blowing his brains out the top of his skull. Then the old man's corpse hit the ground.

CHAPTER FIFTY

The smoke became too thick to breathe as the warehouse burned around June. Her armadillo fists coughed and gagged on the fumes. If she didn't get Tony out of there soon they were going to die of smoke inhalation. But there was one thing standing in her way: Mr. Corpse.

The giant man seemed unfazed by the smoke or fire. June questioned if he was really human, or even a living being.

The concrete club flew at June's head. She ducked and rolled back. Her feet entered a pool of fire as she rolled, covering her shoes in gasoline.

"Fuck!" she cried at the sight of the fire balls dancing on the ends of her legs.

She tried stomping out the fire, but it only caused the gasoline to spread. With Jocko and Judy curled up, she yanked off the shoes and stepped away from them on her bare feet. When she looked down at her armadillos, they were smoking and cringing in pain.

"I'm sorry, babies," she said, blowing the smoke away from their shells.

She looked up at Mr. Corpse. Then she looked down at her fists. She looked at Tony lying on the floor, red ash raining down on him from the ceiling. Then she looked back up at Mr. Corpse.

"Fuck . . ." she said.

There was only one thing she could do. If she wasn't going to run away, she had to stay and fight. And if she had any hope of defeating this monster, she needed to let her demon out. Even if she lost herself in it.

"Come on out, you fucking bitch," she said to herself, to Psycho June.

June didn't want to give in to the demon ever again for a very good reason. It had been taking her over. At first, she was able to release that side of herself only when she wanted to. Only during fights. But before long, her thirst for blood extended out of the ring. When she saw people walking down the street, she wanted to pummel them to death. When she bought food at the convenience store, she wanted to bury her fists in the cashier's skull until the checkout counter was completely painted with chunks of his brain.

It seemed the more she let Psycho June out, the less the bitch wanted to go back in. She didn't want to be restricted anymore. She wanted to play *all* the time.

So June had no other choice. She quit boxing. She locked up Psycho June and threw away the key. And she thought she'd seen the last of the demon until Big Bob's men came after her.

She was afraid of letting the demon out again. If she let it *all* the way out, set it completely free, she doubted she would be able to lock it back up again. She would stay Psycho June for the rest of her life.

But June no longer had a choice. She had to let Psycho June out. It was the only way she could defeat Mr. Corpse and save Tony.

"I'm going to destroy you," she said to Mr. Corpse, as he stomped toward her.

This time she didn't back away as he approached. Her armadillos clenched into tight fists. Her eyes grew red. Her lips curled into a wicked smile. Mr. Corpse no longer looked threatening to her. He looked tasty. She wanted to open him up and feast on his insides.

"You're nothing," she said to Mr. Corpse. "I'm going to obliterate you. Then I'll save the man I love."

As Mr. Corpse raised his concrete club, June clenched her teeth and let Psycho June come all the way out.

"And you're not going to put a single scratch on me," said Psycho June, licking her bloodthirsty lips.

CHAPTER FIFTY-ONE

June was half-dead by the time Tony dragged her out of the burning warehouse.

Blood gushed from over a dozen wounds on her body. Chunks of flesh dangled from her shoulders and chest. Her face was so bloody and swollen that she was no longer recognizable. The side of her head was missing its scalp, exposing a part of her skull. She could barely stand on her legs. Her fists weren't moving, wrapped in a yellow coat.

If Tony hadn't regained consciousness she would have probably died.

"Hang on, Sugar Legs," Tony said. "Mr. Awesome will get you a doctor."

They fell into the yard as the warehouse collapsed behind them. It was a hard battle, but Mr. Corpse was finally dead, buried in a fiery tomb.

June lay in the dirt with a blank look on her face. Psycho June was gone, but it seemed as if she had taken Tony's June along with her. The woman next to him was just a broken, empty shell.

Tony held his wounds as he pulled himself to his stump-legs. Then he found himself staring down a barrel of a gun. A man in a black suit was pointing it at his face. His vision was blurry, so he couldn't tell who it was right away. All he saw was a black suit.

"Mr. Sorry?" Tony asked.

The man in black stepped closer.

"Guess again," he said.

When Tony's eyes focused, he realized it wasn't Mr. Sorry. It was Rape Face. The old man wore a black suit similar to Mr. Sorry's. He'd never seen old Rapey wear black before.

"Sorry is dead," Rape Face said.

CHAPTER FIFTY-TWO

Mr. Sorry rolled Rape Face's corpse into the freshly dug hole. Then he tossed a shovelful of dirt into the old man's wide open eyes, and another onto his raggedy gray suit. When he looked at the next grave over, Mr. Sorry shook a black tear off of his cheek. Then he drove the shovel blade deep into Rape Face's neck, decapitating him.

"That's for Mr. Marathon," Mr. Sorry said, and continued to bury the old bastard.

A gun shot rang out behind him.

Mr. Sorry went limp and fell to the ground.

"Mother fucker," the grumbling voice said behind him.

Rape Face stepped out of the bushes and came toward his body, wearing a black suit. Then another Rape Face came forward, this one wearing a green bowtie. Three more versions of Rape Face came up behind them.

"He's dead," said Bowtie Rape Face, pointing at the gray-suited version of himself in the grave.

"The fucking idiot," said Black Suit Rape Face.

"What are we going to do now?" asked a version of Rape Face standing in the back.

Black Suit Rape Face glared at him. "How the fuck should I know?" Then he pointed at the dead man in the grave. "It was *his* plan."

All five of the Rape Faces spit tobacco juice on the ground at the same time.

When Rape Face went to his doppelganger convention a few years ago, he discovered that every version of himself from every dimension in the universe was exactly the same as he was.

They all looked the same, they all acted the same, they were all basically the exact same person. No matter how different their dimensions were, no matter what path they chose in their lives, each one of them turned out to be the same nasty, bitter, worthless asshole. And every single one of them had the nickname *Rape Face*.

Even though they all completely hated each other, they decided it was in their best interests to team up. Whenever one of them was in trouble, the others would come to his dimension and back him up.

After Big Bob was murdered, Rape Face knew it was a good time to get his dops to come in and help him out. He was going to take over the operation and needed people he could trust. Unfortunately for Rape Face, his dops were just as unreliable as he was. He ended up with a bullet in his head, while they just stood there and watched from a distance.

CHAPTER FIFTY-THREE

"We're splitting up," Rape Face said. "I want you to go with the other guys in the triceratops and keep following Torso. I've got some business to take care of."

"What kind of business?" Mr. Sorry asked.

Rape Face spit tobacco juice as he pulled the T-rex into the gas station. "The kind of business that's none of your fucking business, that's what."

After Mr. Sorry and the others in the triceratops left the gas station, Rape Face called his dops. They had been coming in throughout the night and were now staying at a nearby hotel.

"What?" said one of the Rape Faces.

"It's time to meet up," said Rape Face. "Get everyone together and go to the place I told you about. Now."

"I'm fucking eating a beefsteak sandwich over here," said his dop. "You're gonna have to wait."

"Well gobble that shit down and get your ass over there as fast as you can, you fat fuck," said Rape Face.

"What did you call me, asshole?" said his dop. "You drag me all the way down here to your shitty universe in the middle of the night and you won't even give me ten minutes to let me enjoy a god damned beefsteak? I should cut you."

"Just hurry your ass, motherfucker!" Rape Face yelled.

He smacked his dashboard to turn off the speaker phone, but accidentally left it on.

"Fuckin' prick," his dop said through the phone, thinking he had turned off his speaker phone as well.

When Rape Face turned around, the passenger door to the T-rex opened and Mr. Marathon jumped in.

"What the fuck?" Rape Face said.

Mr. Marathon buckled his seatbelt and stared straight ahead, ready for action.

"Where the fuck did you come from?" Rape Face asked.

Mr. Marathon had a confused look on his face. He regularly had a confused look on his face.

"I was in the bathroom," Marathon said, pointing down at the gas station.

"You were supposed to go with the others in the triceratops."

Mr. Marathon shrugged. "They were gone when I got out, so I thought I was supposed to go with you."

Rape Face banged his head on the controls. "Jesus fuck . . ."

Then the old man started up the dinosaur.

"I guess I'm stuck with your dumb ass then," he said, pulling out of the gas station parking lot to get back on the highway.

Mr. Marathon took off his coat, folded it neatly into a square, and placed it on his lap. Then he folded his hands and put them in the center of his folded coat. Just the thought of sitting next to him pissed Rape Face off.

The old man glared at the young man and sneered when he saw the tattoo on his arm. The number tattooed on Mr. Marathon's arm was number two.

Rape Face wanted to be number two. He was pissed that Big Bob forced him to tattoo the number nine on his back.

"But you don't have a number two," Rape Face would say. "I'm your right hand man. I should be ranked two."

"But you can't fight for shit," Big Bob would reply. "You

think you could take Slick or Sorry? They'd destroy your ass. Hell, even Torso could probably fuck you up. You're lucky you're even number nine."

"Then who's going to be number two then?" Face would ask. "You gotta get somebody for the spot."

"It's none of your damned business who I get. You're not getting number two, so shut the fuck up about it."

But Rape Face never shut the fuck up about it. So, just to piss the ugly bastard off, the boss made Mr. Marathon number two.

Mr. Marathon was the newest, greenest, weakest man in the organization. He really should have been ranked last, but ended up with number two. The boss laughed his ass off when Rape Face found out. The rapey bastard had never been more insulted in his life.

But Big Bob actually liked Mr. Marathon quite a bit. The kid wasn't tough, but he was hard-working and had the right attitude. They called him Mr. Marathon because when he was given a task he didn't rest for a second until it was completed. It didn't matter if the task took an hour, a day, or a week. He stayed focused and worked his ass off until the job was done. Not only that, but he took pride in the work. Even if it was the most tedious job imaginable, he was eager to do it. He was the complete opposite of Rape Face, who bitched and grumbled about doing anything he didn't want to do, even if it would only take a minute.

"Those motherfuckers took long enough," Rape Face grumbled, sitting in his tyrannosaur in the parking lot of a highway diner.

Then he looked over at Mr. Marathon. "Get in the backseat."

Mr. Marathon complied. He was good at taking orders.

"Who are we picking up, Mr. Face?" Marathon asked.

"None of your fucking business," Rape Face said, looking at the five men walking toward the legs of the T-rex.

When Mr. Marathon saw the five Rape Face doppelgangers, a shiver crawled up his back. One Rape Face was bad enough, but being trapped in a dino with five more Rape Faces would be a living hell. When Black Suit Rape Face climbed into the cab, he looked over at Mr. Marathon and said, "Who the fuck is this douchebag?"

It was like Mr. Marathon was seeing double. When Bowtie Rape Face climbed in, Marathon thought he was seeing triple.

"Move the fuck over, ya little prick," Bowtie Rape Face said to Marathon, as he sat next to him in the backseat.

Another Rape Face came in and sat on the other side of him. He was surrounded by Rape Faces.

"Sorry to do this to you kid," Rape Face said, twisting a silencer onto the end of his gun. "But nobody's supposed to know there's more than one of me here."

Mr. Marathon tried to get up, but the two Rape Faces sitting next to him held him in place. Then Rape Face put a pair of bullets in his chest. Two bullets for stealing his number two rank.

CHAPTER FIFTY-FOUR

As Black Suit Rape Face pointed his gun at Tony, the amputee got between him and June.

"Don't shoot her," Tony said, holding his stump-arms out to his sides.

June was lying under the yellow coat on the ground behind him, mumbling to herself, bleeding all over the place.

"Why the fuck shouldn't I?" said Black Suit Rape Face. Then he spit tobacco juice.

"Because you're not the real Mr. Face," Tony said.

The Rape Face was surprised to hear him say that. "How the fuck did you know that?"

Tony pointed his stump at the man's nose. "You don't have the scar."

Rape Face touched his nose.

"While I was giving Mr. Face a ride to the airport, he wouldn't listen to me when I told him that he couldn't smoke in my stegosaur. After the second warning, I slammed on the brakes and his nose got jammed in the cigarette lighter. The burn left a nasty scar on the tip of his nose that you don't have. Plus, I've never seen Mr. Face wearing a suit like the one you got on. It's too expensive."

"Well, clever fucking detective work, jackass," said Black Suit Rape Face. "But I don't give a fuck."

"The point is you don't have any connection to any of this. You can just let us go."

June made gurgling noises.

"Come on," Tony said. "I'm sure we can work out a deal."

Black Suit Rape Face glared at the limbless man. He was thinking it over.

"What kind of deal do you have in mind?" said the rapey doppelganger.

Tony racked his brain, trying to think of what he could offer the man. He didn't have much money saved up. He looked over at June, wondering if she had any savings. But he didn't see much life left in her eyes. Even if she had a fortune saved up, she wouldn't have been able to let him know in her current state. The fight with Mr. Corpse had destroyed her. He wondered if she could ever recover from such serious injuries.

Tony knew he had to do something to save her. Back in the warehouse, when she thought he was unconscious, she had called him *the man she loved*. If she really meant it, if June truly did love Tony even though they hardly knew each other, he couldn't let things end like this. He had to save them both . . . if only to see if they really could have a future together.

CHAPTER FIFTY-FIVE

Tony woke to an intense heat circling around him. When his eyes opened, he saw only ash floating down from the high ceiling like snowflakes.

He had no idea where he was or what was going on. When he looked around, he saw that he was inside of the warehouse. Flames covered the walls. Mr. Happy's corpse lay near him. June was in the center of the room, facing Mr. Corpse with an evil glare in her eyes. When he remembered what had happened last, before the explosion sent him flying through the warehouse window, he was surprised to see Mr. Corpse still alive. Tony had run him over with the stegosaurus and then impaled him on its spiked tail. But there Mr. Corpse was. The long dino spikes remained stuck in his body, but he didn't seem weakened by them. They seemed natural, like the large man wanted them there, like a giant metal spike through his chest was his idea of a body piercing.

Tony watched June as she prepared to fight the monstrosity.

"You're nothing," she said to Mr. Corpse. "I'm going to obliterate you. Then I'll save the man I love."

When she said that last line, Tony's eyes widened. Was *he* the man she loved? He was the only one in the room, so he had to be. He was deeply moved that she felt such a strong connection to him, but he wondered where it had come from. They had had sex and it was good sex, but Tony had good sex with women all the time. His sex partners rarely ever fell in love with him for it. He wondered if there was something else.

June didn't realize Tony was conscious. She was too focused on her opponent, watching him with hungry eyes. Tony could tell she wasn't the same person anymore. She had let her crazy side loose—the same one that he'd seen come out of her when she pulverized Mr. Slick's brains into mush.

Mr. Corpse raised the concrete slab like a baseball bat the size of a rhino's leg. June licked her bloodthirsty lips and charged him. When he swung the club, June ducked and threw a punch with all of her strength.

The beast of a man screamed out in pain. She hadn't hit his body, but one of the stegosaur spikes sticking out of his torso. She punched it on its side, which twisted the spike in his guts. Then she threw an upper-cut into the bottom of another spike. The pain caused the giant hulk to stagger backward through a pool of fire.

He looked back at her. There was a bit of worry in his red eyes. He raised his club again. But once the club was up in the air, a sharp pain went through his chest. The concrete slab dropped down to his flame-coated boots. He wheezed. Then he raised the concrete club again, with a bit of difficulty. His breath was heavy beneath his mask.

June glared at him with her armadillo fists raised. She, too, was breathing heavily. But it wasn't from physical exertion. She breathed heavy with exhilaration.

"Holy crap," Tony said to himself. "She might just be able to beat him . . ."

CHAPTER FIFTY-SIX

Black Suit Rape Face waited for Tony to respond. Tony tried to think of something he could offer the man, but was in too much pain to think straight.

"Don't waste your time," said Black Suit. "You ain't got nothing I want."

Tony waved his arm-stumps.

"You can't kill her," Tony said. "It wasn't her fault."

Black Suit Rape Face chuckled at him and shook his head.

"She killed Big Bob on accident," Tony continued. "He told her to punch him as hard as she could. She just did what he asked."

"You saying he told her to punch him hard enough to kill him?" Rape Face asked with a rapey smile.

"Yeah, something like that."

"I've got news for you, halfy," he said. "That ain't how it happened."

The Rape Face spit tobacco. Tony looked at him with a confused expression.

"What do you mean?" Tony asked.

"That bitch didn't kill the old man," said Black Suit Rape Face. "My dop said so."

"What do you mean?"

"I mean she didn't do it."

CHAPTER FIFTY-SEVEN

Rape Face rubbed his jaw as he ran out of his boss' home gym. He pointed his gun at June as she made her escape, but she ran out the front door before he could fire.

"Fucking bitch," he yelled.

He looked back at his boss. The man whose business he'd been dedicated to for the past twenty years was lying dead on the floor. He wasn't going to let the bitch get away with killing him.

As Rape Face went toward the front entrance, he ran into Mr. Slick, who was standing off to the side, counting his money inside of an envelope.

"Why didn't you stop her?" Rape Face yelled at Mr. Slick.

Mr. Slick shrugged.

Rape Face pointed his gun at the front door. "She just fucking killed the boss you dumb son of a bitch. Get after her."

Rape Face and Mr. Slick ran out of the house into the driveway. Mr. Torso's stegosaur was galloping down the road, away from the house. When Rape Face noticed June was in the passenger seat, he opened fire. Mr. Slick whipped his yo-yo guns out of his coat and joined him, but they were too far away. The stegosaur turned the corner and disappeared.

"What's going on?" said Magic Steve, stepping out of the boss' dino garage and walking down the driveway toward them.

"Armadillo Fists just killed the boss and escaped with Torso," Rape Face said. "I want you to follow them."

"The boss is dead?" asked Magic Steve.

"Just go after them," said Rape Face. "Take the dimetrodon." He turned to the hit man with the yo-yo guns. "Slick, go with him."

Rape Face charged back toward the house.

"Take out both of them if you can," Rape Face said, as Steve and Slick hopped into the dimetrodon. "I'll get the guys together and come after you."

When Rape Face returned to the gym, Big Bob was trying to get to his feet. June hadn't killed him. She just knocked him out, mistaking him for dead when she couldn't feel his pulse through the armadillos.

"What the fuck's going on?" Big Bob said.

He was dizzy and disoriented. He couldn't get himself off the ground.

"You alright, boss?" said Rape Face, trying to help him to his feet. "I thought you were dead."

Big Bob pushed him away. "What the fuck are you doing, you queer. Why am I naked?"

"You were doing your thing with the boxer bitch," said Rape Face. "She knocked you out good."

"Just get away from me," said Big Bob. Then he grumbled to himself, "Worthless sack of shit. Why the hell did I put up with an idiot like you for all these years . . ."

The boss tried to get up on his own, but fell back down. He was weak, helpless.

Rape Face looked down at the old bastard with disgust. He used to look up to him like an older brother. He had a world of respect for the guy. But now, as Big Bob lay naked on the floor, Rape Face just saw him as a pathetic piece of trash. The old man didn't deserve his loyalty or respect. He didn't deserve anything he had.

"Get me my fucking pants," the boss told him, still attempting to get to his feet. "Make yourself useful for a change."

Rape Face went over to the boss' pants, but instead he grabbed the barbell that lay next to them.

"That's not what I asked for, you moron," Big Bob said. "Just get the fuck out of here."

Then Rape Face broke the old man's skull and spread his brains across the mat, making it look like the work of Armadillo Fists, who was well known for splattering the brains of her opponents in the ring.

"*You* get the fuck out of here," he told the corpse. "You're not the boss around here anymore."

Rape Face wiped the blood from his hands and left the room. He had to call Mr. Sorry and gather the men together. But first, he needed to get to an inter-dimensional phone. There were some rapey friends he needed to call.

CHAPTER FIFTY-EIGHT

"So do we keep going with the plan?" asked Bowtie Rape Face, standing over the grave of the real Rape Face. "Or should we just go back home?"

A version of Rape Face with a gold tooth said, "It's fucked. We might as well go home."

A version of Rape Face with a broken nose said, "Yeah, why help a dead guy, right?"

"You guys can go back if you want," said a version of Rape Face with an eye patch. "I'm going to stay here and take his place." He pointed down at the body. All five of them looked at it. "If he's not able to take over his boss' organization then I'm going to. It's better than what I got going for me back home."

"No, you're not, you fucking prick," said Black Suit Rape Face. "If any of us is going to take it over it's going to be *me*."

Gold Tooth Rape Face pulled out his gun. "Like hell you are."

Then all five Rape Faces were pointing their guns at each other. They slowly backed up, trying to aim their guns at all of them at once.

"Wait a minute," said Bowtie Rape Face. "What happened to the dead guy?"

"What fucking dead guy?" said Broken Nose.

"The Sorry motherfucker," Bowtie said.

He pointed at the ground where Mr. Sorry had lain. He was no longer there. They scanned the bushes around them. There wasn't even any blood.

"I thought you shot him?" Eye Patch said to Black Suit.

"I did fucking shoot him," Black Suit said.

"Well, it doesn't look like you did a very good job, you stupid shit," said Gold Tooth.

"Well, he's got to be around here somewhere," Black Suit

said. "Find him."

Then the five Rape Faces spread out.

Mr. Sorry stood in the shadows not twenty feet away, adjusting his glasses and wiping away a black tear.

CHAPTER FIFTY-NINE

While Mr. Food and Mr. Happy put Armadillo Fists in the trunk of the triceratops, Mr. Sorry sat in the passenger seat and got on the speaker phone.

"What?" Rape Face said on the other line.

"We got Armadillo Fists," said Mr. Sorry.

"She dead?" Rape Face asked.

"No," said Mr. Sorry. "Mr. Torso is deceased, but the boxer is unconscious in the trunk. We're about to bring her back to you."

"Did I tell you I wanted you to bring the bitch back to me?" Rape Face said. "Just kill her."

Mr. Sorry replied, "I figured you'd want to find out why she killed the boss."

"I don't give a fuck why she did it. Just do what you're fucking told. Kill the bitch and meet me in an hour."

Rape Face gave him the location of the abandoned warehouse.

"Whatever you say, boss," Mr. Sorry said, wondering why Rape Face wanted her dead so quickly.

"Don't be late," Rape Face said.

Rape Face thought he'd turned the speaker phone off, but as usual he didn't hit the off button properly. Mr. Sorry sat in the triceratops, listening to the old man.

"Was that the Sorry douchebag you were talking about?" someone asked Rape Face on the other line.

"Yeah," Rape Face said. "If we're going to take over the operation he's the first thing that needs to go. I need you guys to get him from behind. Make sure he doesn't see you coming.

That fucker's a slippery bastard and won't die easily."

Mr. Sorry cleaned his glasses with a black silk cloth as he listened to Rape Face's plans. Then he quietly turned off the speaker phone before Mr. Food and Mr. Happy got back into the triceratops.

"So now what?" asked Mr. Food.

"We're going to bring her to Mr. Face," said Mr. Sorry.

Mr. Happy started the dino and got back on the highway.

"Then are we going to kill the bitch?" Mr. Food asked.

"No," said Mr. Sorry. "We're going to keep her alive for a while."

Mr. Sorry stood over Rape Face's corpse. He drove the shovel blade deep into the asshole's neck, decapitating him.

"That's for Mr. Marathon," Mr. Sorry said, and continued to bury the old bastard.

Mr. Sorry heard footsteps coming out of the bushes behind him. He pretended not to notice.

A gun shot rang out behind him.

When he heard the gun shot, he dodged the bullet so fast that his shooter didn't notice. But he reacted as if he'd been shot. He let his body go limp and fell to the ground, feigning death.

Mr. Sorry didn't realize until that moment that the men who were scheming with Rape Face were actually the old bastard's dops. At first, he thought Rape Face had teamed up with a rival organization and was curious to find out which one. But once he found out they were just a group of Rape Faces from alternate dimensions, he realized he didn't have anything to worry about.

He crept away while the five men were arguing, and disappeared into the shadows.

"Well, he's got to be around here somewhere," said the version of Rape Face wearing the black suit. "Fucking find him."

The Rape Faces spread out, hunting him down. But Mr. Sorry wasn't the hunted; he was the hunter. He stood completely silent and motionless, like a praying mantis waiting to strike. He watched calmly as one of them came toward him. A black tear dripped down his cheek.

"What the fuck?" said the Rape Face with the bowtie, looking down at his foot that had just gotten stuck in the mud.

"These are new fucking shoes, asshole," said Bowtie Rape Face to no one in particular. He tried to shake the mud off of his shoe. "Fuck."

As Bowtie Rape Face passed by the shadows where Sorry was lurking, he felt something hit him in the neck. He only saw it for a split second but it looked like a hand with a tattoo of the number three on it. As Bowtie walked on, he realized that he could no longer breathe. His trachea had been crushed. He turned around and searched the shadows he had just passed, but he didn't see anything there. He died trying to figure out why his throat no longer worked.

"You all keep looking for him," said Black Suit Rape Face. "I'll go take care of the others."

Mr. Sorry hovered over the dead man in the bowtie, watching Black Suit as he hiked down the hill toward the burning warehouse.

CHAPTER SIXTY

As Black Suit Rape Face was about to put a bullet in Tony's head, he was interrupted by the sound of gunfire coming from the hills behind the warehouse.

"What the fuck?" said Black Suit, looking in the direction of the gunshots.

When he turned back, Tony flew through the air at him. The human torso kicked the gun out of his hands with his stubby legs, then caught the pistol between his arm-stumps on the way back to the ground.

"How the fuck did you do that with no arms?" cried Black Suit.

"Because I'm awesome," said Mr. Torso. Then he aimed the gun up at the Rape Face. "Now get down on the ground with your hands in the air."

Rape Face didn't comply. "Can you even fire that thing without any fingers?" Then he stepped forward and out-stretched his arm. "Just give it back to me."

Tony tried to fire as the man came at him, but he couldn't pull the trigger with his stumps. The gun slipped out of his arms and hit the ground, causing the gun to go off. Rape Face jumped back as a bullet blew off the top of his shoe, taking two toes with it.

"Motherfucker!" Rape Face yelled, landing on his ass.

Tony retrieved the pistol with his arm-stumps and threw it across the yard, into the fire of the burning warehouse. As the Rape Face in the black suit searched the ground for his missing toes, Tony went for June.

"Come on," he told her. "Let's go."

She got to her feet, but was dizzy and mumbling as though she were severely drunk. Tony helped her balance, leading her in the direction of the triceratops.

"Hurry," he said to her. "There's still time."

But as they staggered across the yard, he examined June's wounds more carefully. Tony wasn't sure if there was enough time to get her to the hospital. She probably wasn't going to make it.

CHAPTER SIXTY-ONE

As June fought Mr. Corpse, Tony wished she hadn't resorted to letting her crazy side loose. He wished she had run away, even if it meant leaving him to burn. The thing about Mr. Corpse was, when he had an opponent in his sights he would not stop until one of them was dead. Psycho June was the same way. Neither of them was capable of backing down from the fight.

Armadillo Fists focused her punches only on the stegosaur spikes in the hulk's chest. She hit them repeatedly, twisting up Mr. Corpse's insides.

"You're going to fucking die," shrieked Psycho June.

Mr. Corpse fell to his knees. June looked down at him with lustful eyes. She licked the man's blood from Jocko's shell. Then she punched him again, bringing all of her weight down on one of the spikes. When it collided, there was a loud ripping noise as the spike tore through the man's flesh. He shoved her away and got to his feet.

"Yeah, you like that?" Psycho June said in a sexy voice, as if she were fighting Big Bob for his erotic pleasure.

Realizing his weakness, Mr. Corpse pulled the metal stegosaurus spikes out of his chest and tossed them to the side. Black blood dribbled slowly from the holes down his muscular abs. Then he raised his club.

"Come on," June said.

When she came at him, Mr. Corpse swung his concrete club at her. It was fast, too fast for her to dodge. It connected with her side and she toppled over. She rolled back to get out of the way, but Mr. Corpse charged her. He swung the concrete upward, nailing her in the chest and face. She flew across the room, through a pool of fire.

Mr. Corpse ran at her and hit her again. This time it ripped flesh from her left shoulder.

June coughed blood across the cement floor. She kicked Mr. Corpse from her prone position. He slammed his concrete club down on her back.

As Tony watched June getting pummeled, it reminded him of a massive chef tenderizing meat with a hammer. He hit her repeatedly, breaking her bones and tearing apart her flesh. But Psycho June didn't cry out. She just laughed as she was battered.

"Is that all you've got?" Psycho June shrieked.

Mr. Corpse smashed her across the face.

"Is that the best you can do?" Psycho June spit a collection of bloody teeth from her mouth.

Tony crawled on his stumps like a dog toward her. He knew he had to try to help. She was just going to let herself die if he didn't. The warehouse was collapsing around them. One side of the roof opened up and an avalanche of flaming wood fell to the floor. There wasn't much time. They were going to soon find themselves buried alive as the warehouse burned to the ground.

CHAPTER SIXTY-TWO

Two Rape Faces came around to the front of the burning warehouse. They walked backward, shooting wildly at the shadows in the distance.

"What the fuck's going on?" asked Black Suit Rape Face, hobbling toward them with his toes in his hand. "I told you to kill that bastard."

The two men turned and ran toward Black Suit.

"That guy's not fucking human," said Gold Tooth Rape Face, reloading his gun.

"He keeps fucking dodging our bullets," said Broken Nose. "What's with that guy?"

"Where are the others?" asked Black Suit.

"Probably dead," said Gold Tooth.

"God damned idiots," said Black Suit. "Just fucking kill the guy."

"Easy for you to say," said Broken Nose. "I'd like to see you go out there and take him out."

Gold Tooth pointed at the two injured people trying to climb into the triceratops. "Yeah, you couldn't even take care of the guy with no arms or legs."

The three men looked over at the vehicle.

"Do something," said Broken Nose. "They're going to get away."

Black Suit pulled out a revolver from an ankle holster beneath his pant leg. "Kill those motherfuckers."

As Tony rolled June into the backseat, he looked back to see the three Rape Faces coming toward them. He crawled into the driver's seat, but then noticed the key wasn't in the ignition.

"Damn it," Tony said.

He had to hotwire it. Working for Bobby Mazetti, this was a skill he had picked up. Unfortunately, without fingers it wasn't something he was very good at. It definitely wasn't something he could do quickly.

The Rape Faces aimed their guns at the triceratops and fired at the hood. Tony ducked down beneath the controls, trying to rip the lower panel off with his mouth.

"Get out of there, legless," said Broken Nose, firing into the triceratops' face.

Tony used his tongue and teeth on the panel, pushing off of the dashboard with his stumps. As it lifted a centimeter, the corner snapped back into place, pinching his tongue. He pulled it back and rubbed his tongue against his stump.

"Damn," Tony said to his tongue. "Come on, don't rush it. Pretend it's a beautiful woman."

Then he slid his tongue beneath the panel, gliding it across the edges, and wiggled the panel free.

The Rape Faces stopped firing. Something else had their attention. As Tony broke the panel off with his teeth, he looked out through the windshield, the panel dangling out of his mouth like a bone in a dog's mouth.

Mr. Sorry walked across the yard toward the Rape Faces, his hands buried in his coat pockets. The Rape Faces left the triceratops and ran for the man with the black tears.

"Kill the son of a bitch," said Black Suit.

The three men surrounded Mr. Sorry on all sides.

"We've got you now, you slimy prick," said Black Suit.

Broken Nose fired first. Mr. Sorry tilted his head and the bullet whizzed past him, hitting Black Suit in the ear.

"You shot me, you fucker!" Black Suit yelled at Broken Nose.

"It's not my fault he moved," said Broken Nose.

"Just kill the fucker," Black Suit said, holding his ear in the same hand containing the severed toes.

All three Rape Faces fired. Mr. Sorry didn't move from his

spot, his hands still in his pockets. He dodged all three bullets, even the one coming from Gold Tooth behind him. One bullet hit Black Suit in his shoulder.

Black Suit cried out and then grumbled at the other two Rape Faces. "Quit missing, you assholes."

"*You* quit missing," said Gold Tooth.

Mr. Sorry looked each of the men in their eyes.

"Please return to your worlds, gentlemen," said Mr. Sorry. "You have no further business here."

"Who the fuck do you think you are?" Black Suit asked him.

Mr. Sorry ignored the question.

"Do you wanna die?" asked Broken Nose.

Mr. Sorry looked at him. "Would *you* like to die?"

"That's what I asked you!" Broken Nose ran at Mr. Sorry, firing at him until his clip was empty.

Mr. Sorry just stared at the man who continued pulling the trigger on the empty gun.

"Is that your answer?" Mr. Sorry asked.

Broken Nose threw a punch at Mr. Sorry, but the man with the black tears ducked out of the way. As Broken Nose threw more punches, Mr. Sorry just avoided them casually, his hands still resting in his pockets.

Black Suit watched Broken Nose fight with all of his strength and not land a single blow. Then Broken Nose froze in place. The life fell out of his eyes. In half a second, Mr. Sorry had pulled his hand out of his pocket, punched Broken Nose in the forehead, and then returned his hand to his pocket. The Rape Faces didn't know what hit him, but they could tell the guy was dead. Mr. Sorry had punched him so hard that his brain hemorrhaged.

Gold Tooth and Black Suit opened fire on Mr. Sorry, but suddenly found Broken Nose's corpse standing between them, blocking the fire. Gold Tooth kept firing into his dead dop, until Mr. Sorry kicked the corpse into him. As Gold Tooth pushed the dead Rape Face to the ground, he realized his gun had been swiped from his hand.

When Gold Tooth looked for where his weapon had gone, he discovered Mr. Sorry had it. But the gun wasn't in Sorry's hand. The man with the black tears still had his hands in his pockets. He was holding the gun with his foot.

In the split second the corpse of Broken Nose landed on Gold Tooth, Mr. Sorry had pulled his foot right out of his shoe, then snatched Gold Tooth's gun away with his toes.

"How the fuck?" Gold Tooth asked.

Mr. Sorry pulled the trigger with his big toe, blowing Gold Tooth's brain out the back of his head. The Rape Face hit the ground. Then Mr. Sorry twirled like a ballerina, aiming the gun at the last Rape Face standing.

"Don't do it," Black Suit Rape Face said. Then he pulled a grenade out of his pocket. "Think you're fast enough to dodge an explosion?"

Mr. Sorry dropped the gun and put his foot back in his shoe below him. He pulled his hands out of his pockets as Rape Face pulled the pin out of the grenade.

"Die you fucker," he said, tossing the grenade at the man with the black tears.

When the grenade was a foot away from his face, Mr. Sorry flicked it with his index finger, sending the grenade over his shoulder. It exploded in the air behind him. Black Suit's face went blank. He backed away from Mr. Sorry in a panic. Mr. Sorry stepped toward him.

"What the fuck's with you?" Rape Face said, pointing his revolver at the man with the black tears.

Then Black Suit heard the sound of an engine revving and turned his head. The triceratops sped across the yard and toward him.

"Motherfuckers," Black Suit yelled.

Before he could aim his revolver, the triceratops plowed into him, knocking him onto the dino's head. Rape Face coughed blood onto the windshield at Tony. Then he looked down to see his torso impaled on the triceratops' horns.

"Legless piece of shit," Rape Face said, wheezing as his intestines spilled out onto the dino's head.

Mr. Sorry approached the triceratops and peered through the window at Tony. The amputee gazed back at the man with the black tears.

"You have my gratitude for killing this man for me," said Mr. Sorry, and then glanced over at the man dying on the triceratops' horns. "Although, I must say it was completely unnecessary."

"I was just trying to help," Tony said.

Mr. Sorry wiped a tear from his eye.

"My apologies for everything we've put you through," said Mr. Sorry. Then he looked back at June lying in the backseat. "Both of you. I know now that it wasn't her fault."

"So you're going to let us go?" Tony asked.

Mr. Sorry nodded. "You also still have a job if you want it. After how well you've proven yourself, I think you deserve a promotion. How's the rank of number four sound?"

Tony shook his head.

"No, thanks," he said. "Besides, I don't think I could handle getting another tattoo. Those things hurt like hell."

Tony smiled. Mr. Sorry smiled back.

"Very well, then," said Mr. Sorry. "You're free to go."

Tony nodded. "Thanks."

Mr. Sorry bowed to him. As he raised his head, giant metal teeth came down from the sky and bit him in half.

"Sorry!" Mr. Torso yelled.

Mr. Sorry's lower half remained standing on the ground. His upper half was missing, replaced by an explosion of blood. When Tony looked out of the window, he saw the tyrannosaurus rex hovering over him. It had Mr. Sorry's upper half in its jaws.

"Where the heck did that come from?" Tony yelled.

Behind the windshield, Tony could see the man operating the controls. It was Rape Face, the one with the eye patch. He was still alive.

The T-rex opened its giant metal jaws and dropped Mr. Sorry's mangled upper half onto the ground. Tony looked down at the pile of flesh that was once the invincible Mr. Sorry. The sight of his mutilated body didn't faze Tony. After what he had just witnessed between June and Mr. Corpse, nothing was going to faze him ever again.

CHAPTER SIXTY-THREE

Tony got to his stump-legs and staggered across the burning warehouse toward Mr. Corpse.

"Hit me harder," Psycho June said to the man hovering over her. "Hit me until I puke!"

Mr. Corpse slammed his concrete slab down into June's stomach.

"Now take your clothes off," she said to him, giggling. "I'll pay you triple!"

Tony jumped at Mr. Corpse and wrapped his stumps around the man's arm, the one holding the club. Mr. Corpse didn't realize it at first. He tried to swing the club, but his arm was too heavy. He looked over at Mr. Torso with red eyes. The limbless man smiled up at him. Then Mr. Corpse tried to shake him off, but Tony held on with all of his strength.

June crawled out from beneath the large man and staggered to her feet.

"I said take your fucking clothes off," Psycho June shrieked, "and let me punch those tight little titties of yours."

She ripped off Mr. Corpse's iron mask and punched him in the face twice.

"Is this hard enough for you?" Psycho June yelled at him as she slammed her armadillos into his head. "Do you like that?"

She put one of her armadillo hands down her boxer shorts and began masturbating. She continued to punch him with the other.

"Harder!" she yelled, licking her bloodthirsty lips as she slammed her fist into him.

Mr. Corpse threw Tony from his arm and slammed him down into the cement. Then he swung his club into June's face. She didn't move. She just stood there and took it. Chunks of meat and gore flew from her cheeks. Blood gushed into her eyes.

"That was an illegal move," Psycho June said, masturbating furiously at him. "But I'll let it slide. I kind of liked it."

Mr. Corpse swung the club again. June ducked. She aimed her armadillo at his wrist.

"*Uh!*" she fake-moaned.

As her fist connected with Mr. Corpse's wrist, the concrete club fell from his hands and broke into pieces as it hit the floor. Then she opened her armadillo fist and grabbed Mr. Corpse's face. He punched her in the chest, but she didn't budge.

"Harder!" she cried.

Psycho June dug her claws deeper into the man's face, and then yanked his head toward her crotch so he could smell the sexual fragrance gushing from her. He punched her again. It only made her masturbate more feverishly.

"Harder!" she cried.

As his blood splashed up her body onto her breasts, she orgasmed. Her battered body jerked against his head, as if she were skull-fucking him. Then she ripped his eyes out of his face. She tossed him to the ground and jumped on top of him. Tony couldn't believe his eyes as the thin girl straddled the hulking beast, dominating him.

"Do you like it?" she said to Mr. Corpse.

Mr. Corpse just gurgled at her. She licked the pulpy mess that was once his face. Then she placed both of her armadillos on his chest and started to dig.

Psycho June giggled as her rabid armadillos burrowed through the man's torso, ripping apart his meat like warm soil. Mr. Corpse screamed so loud it shook the warehouse.

"Feast on his blood," she told her pets. "Pulverize him into soup."

As the fire blazed around her, she arched her back and heaved her breasts forward. After the giant man died, June didn't stop. She rubbed her crotch against his corpse, licking her lips, tasting his flesh through her armadillos' lips.

CHAPTER SIXTY-FOUR

"You're next, halfy!" screamed Eye Patch Rape Face, as he aimed the tyrannosaur's jaws at the triceratops.

Tony slammed on the gas. He didn't have leg-extensions, so he had to stand upright as he drove. He drove the dinosaur around the T-rex's legs to get behind it, as its metal jaws snapped in the air after him.

On the head of the triceratops, Black Suit Rape Face wasn't quite dead yet. He aimed his revolver at Tony and fired, blowing out the windshield. Tony ducked behind the controls as the Rape Face shot at him.

"Die, you prick," Black Suit said.

Tony hit the gas and charged forward, aiming for the T-rex.

"Hold tight, Sugar Legs," Tony said to June.

He looked back. She was no longer moving.

When he was out of bullets, Black Suit began throwing his intestines at Tony, trying to make him crash.

"I'm taking you fucks with me," Rape Face said.

Eye Patch Rape Face laughed madly as he drove the tyrannosaur. He chomped down at the triceratops, biting at the roof.

"I'm going to eat you, you bastards," said Eye Patch, as he controlled the metal jaws of the T-rex.

Tony slammed his triceratops into the tyrannosaur's legs, trying to knock it over.

"You're fucked!" said Black Suit, as he continued throwing his guts at the armless man.

The Rape Face intestines spilled over the side of the dino and got wrapped around one of the triceratops' front legs. As Tony slammed on the gas, the intestines curled around the leg, unraveling from Rape Face's torso.

"You fucking pricks," Black Suit yelled, as the life dropped from his eyes. Then his insides exploded out of his body, spraying across the shattered windshield, and falling beneath the dino's legs.

Rape Face's innards tangled around the vehicle's ankles, but the triceratops' large metal appendages were too strong to be slowed down. The dino plowed forward at full speed, ramming into the side of the tyrannosaur.

"Don't worry, baby," Tony said. "This guy's no match for me. Maybe if I were still driving the stegosaur this guy might have had a bit of an edge, but not in a triceratops."

He patted the dashboard with his stump.

"You see," Tony said, "back when I used to race professionally, I didn't race with a stegosaurus. The vehicle I was most proficient at . . ." Tony spun his dino in a circle, knocking the T-rex off balance, ". . . was the triceratops!"

Then he hit the gas and charged straight into the T-rex, aiming for the carnivore's belly. The horns pierced its abdomen and rammed it backward, pushing the tyrannosaur all the way into the fire of the burning warehouse.

Eye Patch cried out as he fell from the T-rex into the fire. The last thing he saw was the sly expression on Mr. Torso's face as he put on a pair of designer sunglasses with his stubby little arms.

"I guess I was just a little too *awesome* for you," Tony said, smiling and bobbing his head with satisfaction.

But when he looked back at June, she wasn't conscious. The smile fell from his face.

"Sugar Legs?" he asked.

He felt for a pulse with his arm-stump. It was faint. He lifted the yellow coat. The tourniquets wrapped around her wrists had loosened. Blood dripped gently from the shredded meat at the ends of her arms, where her armadillo hands used to be.

CHAPTER SIXTY-FIVE

Tony watched as Psycho June bathed in an orgy of blood. She ripped Mr. Corpse's body into shreds, pulling out his intestines like candy from a piñata.

"June . . ." Tony said, as he stumbled toward her.

When he saw the front of her, he didn't recognize June at all. Her face was swollen and distorted. Blood covered her body. It was like she was turned inside-out. This is what Psycho June looked like on the inside, a demon of blood and cruelty.

As she punched Mr. Corpse's brains into tiny bits, Tony tried to look for traces of the June he knew. But the more he looked, the more he saw only the demon.

"June, come on," he said, going toward her. "We need to get out of here."

As he put his arm-stump on her shoulder, June jerked her head at him. She glared into him with bloodthirsty eyes.

"June?"

She leapt at him. Tony backed away, but she was too fast. She punched him in the stomach, then in the face. He fell to the ground.

"Do you want me to love you?" she said, crawling on top of him. "Do you want me to fuck you with my cock?"

She punched him repeatedly in the chest with her armadillo fists.

"June!" Tony cried.

She continued to punch him.

"These are my cocks," she said, then licked the blood from her fists. "I'm going to fuck you with them. I'm going to make you love me."

"Stop it!" he said to the demon on top of him.

She kept punching, grinding her crotch against his limbless torso.

"Is that hard enough for you?" she said. "Or should I fuck you even harder?"

She punched him in the face and blood sprayed from his nose.

"June . . ." he said.

As she licked the shell of her armadillo, part of the warehouse crashed down behind her, awakening her from her trance. When she looked down at Tony squirming beneath her, her lips began to tremble. Tears fell from her swollen eyes, mixing with the blood.

She screamed and crawled off of him. Then she turned away, covering her face with her armadillos.

"It's okay," Tony said, sitting upright. "I know you didn't mean it. It wasn't you."

She cried and quivered.

"You're wrong," June said. "It *was* me. I *wanted* to do all of those things."

"No, you didn't," Tony said, staggering toward her.

June put her fist between them.

"Stay back," she said. "Even now, there's a part of me that wants nothing more than to smash your skull into the cement. I *long* for it." She ground her teeth. "It makes me wet just thinking about it."

Tony wrapped his stumps around her. He didn't care if the smoke suffocated them. He didn't care if the warehouse crumbled down on their heads. He just had to comfort her. At that moment, it was the most important thing he could possibly do.

"It's okay," Tony said. "I don't care what you say. It's not your fault."

He looked up into her crooked eyes and smiled.

"You just need help," he said. "Let me help you."

But all he saw in her eyes was a fire, a thirst for blood.

"No," she said.

Psycho June was back.

"There's only one thing I need," said Psycho June.

She pushed Tony out of the way and raised her fists to him. But instead of attacking him, she turned on herself. She opened

143

her armadillo, Jocko, and had him bite down into her other wrist.

"Don't!" Tony yelled.

June and Psycho June screamed together as Jocko chewed through her arm. It severed Judy, her other armadillo, from her wrist. Blood gushed out of the mangled stump, fizzing in the pool of fire by her feet.

"Stop!" Tony cried, catching her severed armadillo before it hit the ground.

Then June went to the fragmented concrete slab that Mr. Corpse had used as a club. She picked out a jagged piece of it, sharp like the edge of an axe.

"June . . ."

She shrieked as she slammed her wrist down on the edge of the concrete, breaking open her flesh. Blood sprayed across the floor. She slammed it again, then again.

When Tony reached her, Jocko was dangling from a strip of flesh, squirming and trying to reattach itself to June's arm. But Psycho June wouldn't let it. She opened her crooked jaws and bit down on the hunk of meat between her armadillo and her wrist. Tony caught Jocko with his stumps after she finished chewing through her flesh.

Then June collapsed to her knees, crying. Blood poured out of her stumps, pooling on the ground below her.

"It's okay," Tony said to her.

He ripped strips from his orange spandex shirt and wrapped them around her wrists. The tourniquets cut off the blood flow, preventing her from bleeding to death. Then he took Mr. Happy's coat off, wrapped up the armadillos and placed them in June's arms.

"You didn't have to do this," Tony said to June as he helped her to her feet.

She was getting dizzy.

"I did," she said, her eyes rolling back as she shook her head. "It was the only way to save you."

As they staggered out of the burning warehouse, she mumbled under her breath, "The temptation was just too great."

CHAPTER SIXTY-SIX

The triceratops galloped down the highway at top speed, leaping over every dino that got in its way. Tony looked back at June. The armadillos crawled on her shoulders, licking the wounds on her face.

"Come on, Mr. Awesome," Tony said to himself. "You can make it."

As the armadillos tickled her cheeks, June giggled. Her eyes blinked open.

"Jocko, Judy," she said in a languid voice. "How are my babies?"

She closed her eyes and nuzzled her swollen face against them, smiling. Then she looked at Tony.

"My babies are moving on their own," she said to Tony. "They never listen to me."

She raised an arm out from under the yellow coat and saw the bloody stump.

"Oh . . ." she said, remembering what had happened.

The smile fell from her face.

"Don't worry," Tony said to her. "I'll get you to the hospital in time. Just hang in there."

June dropped her arm and smiled again.

"Mr. Fast Awesome . . ." she said, giggling.

Then she looked down at her arm stumps.

"I want to be *Mrs.* Fast Awesome," she said. "You can teach me how to get around with no hands. Then we can be a team. Maybe I'll even cut my legs off, too, right at the knee. We'll be the perfect pair."

She laughed at the thought.

"Who needs arms or legs to be happy," she said. "You taught me that. You're the most awesome man I've ever met."

"You know it, Sugar Legs," Tony said, trying to keep her

talking. "Tell me more about how awesome I am."

June laid her head on Jocko's back, snuggling his shell.

"You're the epitome of awesome," she said. "You're the fastest driver, the smoothest talker, the only person in the world who can make orange spandex look sexy."

Tony winked at her through the rearview mirror.

"When you make love to me it makes me feel like I'm the center of the universe." Her eyes stared out the window for a moment, admiring the sun as it rose over the horizon. "I've never felt that way before. I want to feel that way again."

"Hang in there, June," Tony said. "I'll make you feel that way everyday if you want. Just hang on."

"I want to have babies with you, Mr. Awesome," June said.

Tony could tell she was getting really delirious.

She said, "I bet you'd be the best father. I'd love to see you surrounded by Baby Awesomes." She giggled. "And I'd be there with Jocko and Judy. They'd be our family pets. It would be so perfect."

Her eyes began to fade.

"So perfect . . ." she said.

Tony looked back at her.

"I said hang in there," he said. "Keep talking."

The smile drifted from her face.

"I've got to go faster," he said.

Tony pushed the gas all the way down, speeding up as fast as the triceratops could take him, leaping over ankylosaurs and trachodons. He looked back. June's head fell from Jocko's shell and dangled in the air over her chest. Tears poured from his eyes as he turned back to face the road.

"I'm not fast enough," Tony said, as he plowed past everyone on the road. "Why am I not fast enough?"

He wanted to look back and see her smiling at him again. Just one last time. But he couldn't. He had to keep his eyes on the road. He had to go faster, even faster than he'd ever gone before. He couldn't look back at her. He knew she wasn't moving anymore. The blood was no longer dripping from her body.

CHAPTER SIXTY-SEVEN

Tony looked back at June as she stepped into his stegosaurus. She sat in the backseat, hiding her armadillo fists inside her jacket pockets. As he pulled into dinosaur traffic, he looked at her through the rearview mirror. She had a pretty face and a bashful smile.

"What's a sweet girl like you doing working for a jerk like Big Bob?" Tony asked.

Their eyes met in the rearview mirror. She smiled and looked away.

"I'm not as sweet as you think I am," June said.

"Fair enough," Tony said. "So what's he got you doing for him?"

"I think he needs a personal trainer," June said. "Or something like that. I used to be a boxer. He admired my skills."

"A boxer?" Tony asked. "A pretty little thing like you?"

"I was a killer," she said.

Then June noticed that her driver didn't have any arms.

"What happened?" she asked him, nodding at his missing limbs.

Tony raised his stumps. "Dinosaur crash when I was young. I lost both my arms and legs."

"You're a professional driver even though you were in such a horrible accident?" June said. "If that happened to me I'd never step foot in a dinosaur again."

"Not me, baby," Tony said. "It only made me want to drive more. If somebody tells me I'm not able to do something I don't just want to do it, I want to be the best at it."

"So you're the best driver in Big Bob's organization?" she asked.

"Not just in the organization," Tony said. "I'm the best driver. Period. Nobody goes as fast as me."

He winked in the rearview mirror.

"I like going fast," June said.

"Want me to speed up, baby?" he said.

"No, thanks," she said. "I'm not in a rush."

"I hear you," Tony said.

He raised his arm-stump over the seat. "The name's Tony."

She pulled an armadillo out of her pocket and wrapped it around his stump.

"June," she said.

When he shook her armadillo hand, June was surprised it didn't bother him. He didn't cringe or react in any way, as if it were completely natural for women to have armadillo hands.

"A pleasure to meet you, Sugar Doll," Tony said.

She nodded at him as she returned her hand to her pocket. Then she went silent, staring out the window at all the metal dinosaurs they passed.

As they drove, Tony sensed something in her. He sensed loneliness—a deep, crushing loneliness that had been consuming her for a very long time. It was as if there was a hole in her that she kept trying to fill, but she was always filling it with the wrong thing.

It made Tony sad to think that such a sweet girl was always hurting inside. He wanted to do something to help her. He didn't know what. He just didn't want her to be so empty anymore.

Tony smiled at her in the rearview mirror. She didn't smile back. Her eyes were distant.

When he dropped her off at the boss' house, she looked at him through the passenger side window.

"You going to drive me home after I'm done?" she asked.

Tony nodded. "I'll be waiting right here."

"Do you always just wait around for your passengers?"

Tony shook his head. "Just for you, Sugar Legs."

She nodded and turned around. He watched her as she walked away from him, up the driveway, into the belly of the beast.

If he knew what Big Bob had planned for her, or what would happen to her after she was blamed for the old man's death, Tony wouldn't have dropped her off that day. He would have slammed on the gas and kept driving, taking her as far away from there as possible, to a place where she would never have to use her fists ever again.

CHAPTER SIXTY-EIGHT

A week after June Howard's funeral, Tony took a road trip up to the mountains. He didn't drive himself. He decided he wanted to be a passenger for a change, riding in the back of a parasaur taxi.

"Pull over up here," Tony said to the cabby.

The cabby looked back at him as if he were crazy.

"You want me to drop you off here?" the cabby asked. "It's the middle of nowhere."

"Yeah, right here," Tony said.

The cabby shrugged as he pulled the dino onto the side of the road.

"You sure you're going to be okay out here?" said the cabby. "I mean, you don't even have any arms or legs."

"Don't need 'em," Tony said, as he jumped out of the cab. "I'll be fine."

Tony paid the cabby and then watched as the parasaur walked slowly on its way down the road. Then he turned to the wilderness. He wobbled down a hill, trying to balance on his stubby legs. Then he hiked away from the road, to a quiet, peaceful spot. He sat down on a patch of grass and poured himself a glass of wine.

June's funeral was small. Not many people were there: a couple uncles and cousins she barely knew, a childhood friend who hadn't seen her in years, a next door neighbor who spoke to her sometimes.

Tony placed a small animal cage in front of him and opened it with his teeth. Then he slid his arm-stumps within. As Jocko and Judy crawled up his half-limbs to his shoulders, he giggled.

"Your claws are sure tickly," he told them.

Then he pulled them off of his shoulder one by one and held them in his arms like babies.

"I'm happy the vet was able to fix you up," he said to them, tapping Judy on her nose as she licked his stump. "Now you're able to be normal armadillos again."

He set them on the ground.

"Now be a good boy, Jocko," he said to June's right fist. "Protect your sister for me."

Then he turned to June's left fist. "And Judy, make sure to brighten your brother's day. He gets a little moody sometimes. Cheer him up when you can."

The armadillos stared up at him, licking their noses with their sticky tongues. They seemed sad when Tony waved them away with his arm-stumps.

"You're free," he said. "Go explore. There's a big world out there with your names on it."

Tony sat in the grass, drinking his wine, and watched as the armadillos disappeared into the brush. He smiled thinking of June.

It was going to take a long time for him to get over their owner's death, but it eased his pain a little to know that a part of June lived on inside of those two armadillos. Just as they existed as a part of her body, she would continue to exist as a part of theirs. And because the armadillos had each other, June would never be lonely again.

After he finished the wine and absorbed all the warmth from the sun, Tony stood up on his stubby legs. He put on his hat and designer sunglasses.

"Come on, Mr. Awesome," he said to himself. "There's a big world out there with your name on it."

Then he hiked up the hill, back to the road. He chose a direction and started walking. He didn't know where he was going. He just wanted to walk and keep walking, to see just how far a man with no legs could travel.

ABOUT THE AUTHOR

Carlton Mellick III is one of the leading authors of the bizarro fiction subgenre. Since 2001, his books have drawn an international cult following, despite the fact that they have been shunned by most libraries and chain bookstores.

He won the Wonderland Book Award for his novel, *Warrior Wolf Women of the Wasteland*, in 2009. His short fiction has appeared in *Vice Magazine, The Year's Best Fantasy and Horror #16, The Magazine of Bizarro Fiction,* and *Zombies: Encounters with the Hungry Dead*, among others. He is also a graduate of Clarion West, where he studied under the likes of Chuck Palahniuk, Connie Willis, and Cory Doctorow.

He lives in Portland, OR, the bizarro fiction mecca.

Visit him online at **www.carltonmellick.com**

Bizarro Books

CATALOG FALL 2011

ERASERHEAD
PRESS

Your major resource for the bizarro fiction genre:

WWW.BIZARROCENTRAL.COM

Introduce yourselves to the bizarro fiction genre and all of its authors with the Bizarro Starter Kit series. Each volume features short novels and short stories by ten of the leading bizarro authors, designed to give you a perfect sampling of the genre for only $10.

BB-0X1
"The Bizarro Starter Kit"
(Orange)
Featuring D. Harlan Wilson, Carlton Mellick III, Jeremy Robert Johnson, Kevin L Donihe, Gina Ranalli, Andre Duza, Vincent W. Sakowski, Steve Beard, John Edward Lawson, and Bruce Taylor.
236 pages $10

BB-0X2
"The Bizarro Starter Kit"
(Blue)
Featuring Ray Fracalossy, Jeremy C. Shipp, Jordan Krall, Mykle Hansen, Andersen Prunty, Eckhard Gerdes, Bradley Sands, Steve Aylett, Christian TeBordo, and Tony Rauch. **244 pages $10**

BB-0X2
"The Bizarro Starter Kit"
(Purple)
Featuring Russell Edson, Athena Villaverde, David Agranoff, Matthew Revert, Andrew Goldfarb, Jeff Burk, Garrett Cook, Kris Saknussemm, Cody Goodfellow, and Cameron Pierce **264 pages $10**

BB-001 **"The Kafka Effekt" D. Harlan Wilson** — A collection of forty-four irreal short stories loosely written in the vein of Franz Kafka, with more than a pinch of William S. Burroughs sprinkled on top. **211 pages $14**

BB-002 **"Satan Burger" Carlton Mellick III** — The cult novel that put Carlton Mellick III on the map ... Six punks get jobs at a fast food restaurant owned by the devil in a city violently overpopulated by surreal alien cultures. **236 pages $14**

BB-003 **"Some Things Are Better Left Unplugged" Vincent Sakwoski** — Join The Man and his Nemesis, the obese tabby, for a nightmare roller coaster ride into this postmodern fantasy. **152 pages $10**

BB-004 **"Shall We Gather At the Garden?" Kevin L Donihe** — Donihe's Debut novel. Midgets take over the world, The Church of Lionel Richie vs. The Church of the Byrds, plant porn and more! **244 pages $14**

BB-005 **"Razor Wire Pubic Hair" Carlton Mellick III** — A genderless humandildo is purchased by a razor dominatrix and brought into her nightmarish world of bizarre sex and mutilation. **176 pages $11**

BB-006 **"Stranger on the Loose" D. Harlan Wilson** — The fiction of Wilson's 2nd collection is planted in the soil of normalcy, but what grows out of that soil is a dark, witty, otherworldly jungle... **228 pages $14**

BB-007 **"The Baby Jesus Butt Plug" Carlton Mellick III** — Using clones of the Baby Jesus for anal sex will be the hip sex fetish of the future. **92 pages $10**

BB-008 **"Fishyfleshed" Carlton Mellick III** — The world of the past is an illogical flatland lacking in dimension and color, a sick-scape of crispy squid people wandering the desert for no apparent reason. **260 pages $14**

BB-009 "Dead Bitch Army" Andre Duza — Step into a world filled with racist teenagers, cannibals, 100 warped Uncle Sams, automobiles with razor-sharp teeth, living graffiti, and a pissed-off zombie bitch out for revenge. **344 pages $16**

BB-010 "The Menstruating Mall" Carlton Mellick III — "The Breakfast Club meets Chopping Mall as directed by David Lynch." - Brian Keene **212 pages $12**

BB-011 "Angel Dust Apocalypse" Jeremy Robert Johnson — Methheads, man-made monsters, and murderous Neo-Nazis. "Seriously amazing short stories..." - Chuck Palahniuk, author of Fight Club **184 pages $11**

BB-012 "Ocean of Lard" Kevin L Donihe / Carlton Mellick III — A parody of those old Choose Your Own Adventure kid's books about some very odd pirates sailing on a sea made of animal fat. **176 pages $12**

BB-015 "Foop!" Chris Genoa — Strange happenings are going on at Dactyl, Inc, the world's first and only time travel tourism company.
"A surreal pie in the face!" - Christopher Moore **300 pages $14**

BB-020 "Punk Land" Carlton Mellick III — In the punk version of Heaven, the anarchist utopia is threatened by corporate fascism and only Goblin, Mortician's sperm, and a blue-mohawked female assassin named Shark Girl can stop them. **284 pages $15**

BB-027 "Siren Promised" Jeremy Robert Johnson & Alan M Clark — Nominated for the Bram Stoker Award. A potent mix of bad drugs, bad dreams, brutal bad guys, and surreal/incredible art by Alan M. Clark. **190 pages $13**

BB-031"Sea of the Patchwork Cats" Carlton Mellick III — A quiet dreamlike tale set in the ashes of the human race. For Mellick enthusiasts who also adore The Twilight Zone. **112 pages $10**

BB-032 **"Extinction Journals" Jeremy Robert Johnson** — An uncanny voyage across a newly nuclear America where one man must confront the problems associated with loneliness, insane dieties, radiation, love, and an ever-evolving cockroach suit with a mind of its own. **104 pages $10**

BB-037 **"The Haunted Vagina" Carlton Mellick III** — It's difficult to love a woman whose vagina is a gateway to the world of the dead. **132 pages $10**

BB-043 **"War Slut" Carlton Mellick III** — Part "1984," part "Waiting for Godot," and part action horror video game adaptation of John Carpenter's "The Thing." **116 pages $10**

BB-047 **"Sausagey Santa" Carlton Mellick III** — A bizarro Christmas tale featuring Santa as a piratey mutant with a body made of sausages. 124 pages $10

BB-048 **"Misadventures in a Thumbnail Universe" Vincent Sakowski** — Dive deep into the surreal and satirical realms of neo-classical Blender Fiction, filled with television shoes and flesh-filled skies. **120 pages $10**

BB-053 **"Ballad of a Slow Poisoner" Andrew Goldfarb** — Millford Mutterwurst sat down on a Tuesday to take his afternoon tea, and made the unpleasant discovery that his elbows were becoming flatter. **128 pages $10**

BB-055 **"Help! A Bear is Eating Me" Mykle Hansen** — The bizarro, heartwarming, magical tale of poor planning, hubris and severe blood loss... **150 pages $11**

BB-056 **"Piecemeal June" Jordan Krall** — A man falls in love with a living sex doll, but with love comes danger when her creator comes after her with crab-squid assassins. **90 pages $9**

BB-058 **"The Overwhelming Urge" Andersen Prunty** — A collection of bizarro tales by Andersen Prunty. **150 pages $11**

BB-059 **"Adolf in Wonderland" Carlton Mellick III** — A dreamlike adventure that takes a young descendant of Adolf Hitler's design and sends him down the rabbit hole into a world of imperfection and disorder. **180 pages $11**

BB-061 **"Ultra Fuckers" Carlton Mellick III** — Absurdist suburban horror about a couple who enter an upper middle class gated community but can't find their way out. **108 pages $9**

BB-062 **"House of Houses" Kevin L. Donihe** — An odd man wants to marry his house. Unfortunately, all of the houses in the world collapse at the same time in the Great House Holocaust. Now he must travel to House Heaven to find his departed fiancee. **172 pages $11**

BB-064 **"Squid Pulp Blues" Jordan Krall** — In these three bizarro-noir novellas, the reader is thrown into a world of murderers, drugs made from squid parts, deformed gun-toting veterans, and a mischievous apocalyptic donkey. **204 pages $12**

BB-065 **"Jack and Mr. Grin" Andersen Prunty** — "When Mr. Grin calls you can hear a smile in his voice. Not a warm and friendly smile, but the kind that seizes your spine in fear. You don't need to pay your phone bill to hear it. That smile is in every line of Prunty's prose." - Tom Bradley. **208 pages $12**

BB-066 **"Cybernetrix" Carlton Mellick III** — What would you do if your normal everyday world was slowly mutating into the video game world from Tron? **212 pages $12**

BB-072 **"Zerostrata" Andersen Prunty** — Hansel Nothing lives in a tree house, suffers from memory loss, has a very eccentric family, and falls in love with a woman who runs naked through the woods every night. **144 pages $11**

BB-073 "The Egg Man" Carlton Mellick III — It is a world where humans reproduce like insects. Children are the property of corporations, and having an enormous ten-foot brain implanted into your skull is a grotesque sexual fetish. Mellick's industrial urban dystopia is one of his darkest and grittiest to date. **184 pages $11**

BB-074 "Shark Hunting in Paradise Garden" Cameron Pierce — A group of strange humanoid religious fanatics travel back in time to the Garden of Eden to discover it is invested with hundreds of giant flying maneating sharks. **150 pages $10**

BB-075 "Apeshit" Carlton Mellick III - Friday the 13th meets Visitor Q. Six hipster teens go to a cabin in the woods inhabited by a deformed killer. An incredibly fucked-up parody of B-horror movies with a bizarro slant. **192 pages $12**

BB-076 "Fuckers of Everything on the Crazy Shitting Planet of the Vomit At smosphere" Mykle Hansen - Three bizarro satires. Monster Cocks, Journey to the Center of Agnes Cuddlebottom, and Crazy Shitting Planet. **228 pages $12**

BB-077 "The Kissing Bug" Daniel Scott Buck — In the tradition of Roald Dahl, Tim Burton, and Edward Gorey, comes this bizarro anti-war children's story about a bohemian conenose kissing bug who falls in love with a human woman. **116 pages $10**

BB-078 "MachoPoni" Lotus Rose — It's My Little Pony... *Bizarro* style! A long time ago Poniworld was split in two. On one side of the Jagged Line is the Pastel Kingdom, a magical land of music, parties, and positivity. On the other side of the Jagged Line is Dark Kingdom inhabited by an army of undead ponies. **148 pages $11**

BB-079 "The Faggiest Vampire" Carlton Mellick III — A Roald Dahl-esque children's story about two faggy vampires who partake in a mustache competition to find out which one is truly the faggiest. **104 pages $10**

BB-080 "Sky Tongues" Gina Ranalli — The autobiography of Sky Tongues, the biracial hermaphrodite actress with tongues for fingers. Follow her strange life story as she rises from freak to fame. **204 pages $12**

BB-081 **"Washer Mouth" Kevin L. Donihe** - A washing machine becomes human and pursues his dream of meeting his favorite soap opera star. **244 pages $11**

BB-082 **"Shatnerquake" Jeff Burk** - All of the characters ever played by William Shatner are suddenly sucked into our world. Their mission: hunt down and destroy the real William Shatner. **100 pages $10**

BB-083 **"The Cannibals of Candyland" Carlton Mellick III** - There exists a race of cannibals that are made of candy. They live in an underground world made out of candy. One man has dedicated his life to killing them all. **170 pages $11**

BB-084 **"Slub Glub in the Weird World of the Weeping Willows"** **Andrew Goldfarb** - The charming tale of a blue glob named Slub Glub who helps the weeping willows whose tears are flooding the earth. There are also hyenas, ghosts, and a voodoo priest **100 pages $10**

BB-085 **"Super Fetus" Adam Pepper** - Try to abort this fetus and he'll kick your ass! **104 pages $10**

BB-086 **"Fistful of Feet" Jordan Krall** - A bizarro tribute to spaghetti westerns, featuring Cthulhu-worshipping Indians, a woman with four feet, a crazed gunman who is obsessed with sucking on candy, Syphilis-ridden mutants, sexually transmitted tattoos, and a house devoted to the freakiest fetishes. **228 pages $12**

BB-087 **"Ass Goblins of Auschwitz" Cameron Pierce** - It's Monty Python meets Nazi exploitation in a surreal nightmare as can only be imagined by Bizarro author Cameron Pierce. **104 pages $10**

BB-088 **"Silent Weapons for Quiet Wars" Cody Goodfellow** - "This is high-end psychological surrealist horror meets bottom-feeding low-life crime in a techno-thrilling science fiction world full of Lovecraft and magic..." -John Skipp **212 pages $12**

BB-089 "Warrior Wolf Women of the Wasteland" Carlton Mellick III
— Road Warrior Werewolves versus McDonaldland Mutants...post-apocalyptic fiction has never been quite like this. **316 pages $13**

BB-091 "Super Giant Monster Time" Jeff Burk
— A tribute to choose your own adventures and Godzilla movies. Will you escape the giant monsters that are rampaging the fuck out of your city and shit? Or will you join the mob of alien-controlled punk rockers causing chaos in the streets? What happens next depends on you. **188 pages $12**

BB-092 "Perfect Union" Cody Goodfellow
— "Cronenberg's THE FLY on a grand scale: human/insect gene-spliced body horror, where the human hive politics are as shocking as the gore." -John Skipp. **272 pages $13**

BB-093 "Sunset with a Beard" Carlton Mellick III
— 14 stories of surreal science fiction. **200 pages $12**

BB-094 "My Fake War" Andersen Prunty
— The absurd tale of an unlikely soldier forced to fight a war that, quite possibly, does not exist. It's Rambo meets Waiting for Godot in this subversive satire of American values and the scope of the human imagination. **128 pages $11**

BB-095 "Lost in Cat Brain Land" Cameron Pierce
— Sad stories from a surreal world. A fascist mustache, the ghost of Franz Kafka, a desert inside a dead cat. Primordial entities mourn the death of their child. The desperate serve tea to mysterious creatures. A hopeless romantic falls in love with a pterodactyl. And much more. **152 pages $11**

BB-096 "The Kobold Wizard's Dildo of Enlightenment +2" Carlton Mellick III
— A Dungeons and Dragons parody about a group of people who learn they are only made up characters in an AD&D campaign and must find a way to resist their nerdy teenaged players and retarded dungeon master in order to survive. **232 pages $12**

BB-098 "A Hundred Horrible Sorrows of Ogner Stump" Andrew Goldfarb
— Goldfarb's acclaimed comic series. A magical and weird journey into the horrors of everyday life. **164 pages $11**

BB-099 **"Pickled Apocalypse of Pancake Island" Cameron Pierce**—A demented fairy tale about a pickle, a pancake, and the apocalypse. **102 pages $8**

BB-100 **"Slag Attack" Andersen Prunty**— Slag Attack features four visceral, noir stories about the living, crawling apocalypse.A slag is what survivors are calling the slug-like maggots raining from the sky, burrowing inside people, and hollowing out their flesh and their sanity. **148 pages $11**

BB-101 **"Slaughterhouse High" Robert Devereaux**—A place where schools are built with secret passageways, rebellious teens get zippers installed in their mouths and genitals, and once a year, on that special night, one couple is slaughtered and the bits of their bodies are kept as souvenirs. **304 pages $13**

BB-102 **"The Emerald Burrito of Oz" John Skipp & Marc Levinthal** —OZ IS REAL! Magic is real! The gate is really in Kansas! And America is finally allowing Earth tourists to visit this weird-ass, mysterious land. But when Gene of Los Angeles heads off for summer vacation in the Emerald City, little does he know that a war is brewing...a war that could destroy both worlds. **280 pages $13**

BB-103 **"The Vegan Revolution... with Zombies" David Agranoff** — When there's no more meat in hell, the vegans will walk the earth. **160 pages $11**

BB-104 **"The Flappy Parts" Kevin L Donihe**—Poems about bunnies, LSD, and police abuse. You know, things that matter. 132 **pages $11**

BB-105 **"Sorry I Ruined Your Orgy" Bradley Sands**—Bizarro humorist Bradley Sands returns with one of the strangest, most hilarious collections of the year. **130 pages $11**

BB-106 **"Mr. Magic Realism" Bruce Taylor**—Like Golden Age science fiction comics written by Freud, *Mr. Magic Realism* is a strange, insightful adventure that spans the furthest reaches of the galaxy, exploring the hidden caverns in the hearts and minds of men, women, aliens, and biomechanical cats. **152 pages $11**

BB-107 **"Zombies and Shit" Carlton Mellick III**—"Battle Royale" meets "Return of the Living Dead." Mellick's bizarro tribute to the zombie genre. **308 pages $13**

BB-108 **"The Cannibal's Guide to Ethical Living" Mykle Hansen**— Over a five star French meal of fine wine, organic vegetables and human flesh, a lunatic delivers a witty, chilling, disturbingly sane argument in favor of eating the rich.. **184 pages $11**

BB-109 **"Starfish Girl" Athena Villaverde**—In a post-apocalyptic underwater dome society, a girl with a starfish growing from her head and an assassin with sea anenome hair are on the run from a gang of mutant fish men. **160 pages $11**

BB-110 **"Lick Your Neighbor" Chris Genoa**—Mutant ninjas, a talking whale, kung fu masters, maniacal pilgrims, and an alcoholic clown populate Chris Genoa's surreal, darkly comical and unnerving reimagining of the first Thanksgiving. **303 pages $13**

BB-111 **"Night of the Assholes" Kevin L. Donihe**—A plague of assholes is infecting the countryside. Normal everyday people are transforming into jerks, snobs, dicks, and douchebags. And they all have only one purpose: to make your life a living hell.. **192 pages $11**

BB-112 **"Jimmy Plush, Teddy Bear Detective" Garrett Cook**—Hardboiled cases of a private detective trapped within a teddy bear body. **180 pages $11**

BB-113 **"The Deadheart Shelters" Forrest Armstrong**—The hip hop lovechild of William Burroughs and Dali... **144 pages $11**

BB-114 **"Eyeballs Growing All Over Me... Again" Tony Raugh**— Absurd, surreal, playful, dream-like, whimsical, and a lot of fun to read. **144 pages $11**

BB-115 **"Whargoul" Dave Brockie** — From the killing grounds of Stalingrad to the death camps of the holocaust. From torture chambers in Iraq to race riots in the United States, the Whargoul was there, killing and raping. **244 pages $12**

BB-116 **"By the Time We Leave Here, We'll Be Friends" J. David Osborne** — A David Lynchian nightmare set in a Russian gulag, where its prisoners, guards, traitors, soldiers, lovers, and demons fight for survival and their own rapidly deteriorating humanity. **168 pages $11**

BB-117 **"Christmas on Crack" edited by Carlton Mellick III** — Perverted Christmas Tales for the whole family! . . . as long as every member of your family is over the age of 18. **168 pages $11**

BB-118 **"Crab Town" Carlton Mellick III** — Radiation fetishists, balloon people, mutant crabs, sail-bike road warriors, and a love affair between a woman and an H-Bomb. This is one mean asshole of a city. Welcome to Crab Town. **100 pages $8**

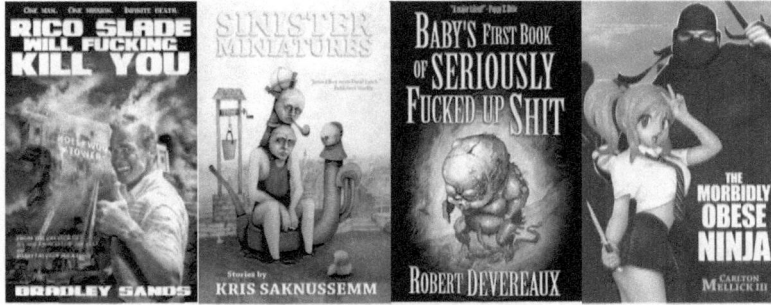

BB-119 **"Rico Slade Will Fucking Kill You" Bradley Sands** — Rico Slade is an action hero. Rico Slade can rip out a throat with his bare hands. Rico Slade's favorite food is the honey-roasted peanut. Rico Slade will fucking kill everyone. A novel. **122 pages $8**

BB-120 **"Sinister Miniatures" Kris Saknussemm** — The definitive collection of short fiction by Kris Saknussemm, confirming that he is one of the best, most daring writers of the weird to emerge in the twenty-first century. **180 pages $11**

BB-121 **"Baby's First Book of Seriously Fucked up Shit" Robert Devereaux** — Ten stories of the strange, the gross, and the just plain fucked up from one of the most original voices in horror. **176 pages $11**

BB-122 **"The Morbidly Obese Ninja" Carlton Mellick III** — These days, if you want to run a successful company . . . you're going to need a lot of ninjas. **92 pages $8**

BB-123 **"Abortion Arcade" Cameron Pierce** — An intoxicating blend of body horror and midnight movie madness, reminiscent of early David Lynch and the splatterpunks at their most sublime. **172 pages $11**

BB-124 "Black Hole Blues" Patrick Wensink — A hilarious double helix of country music and physics. **196 pages $11**

BB-125 "Barbarian Beast Bitches of the Badlands" Carlton Mellick III — Three prequels and sequels to *Warrior Wolf Women of the Wasteland.* **284 pages $13**

BB-126 "The Traveling Dildo Salesman" Kevin L. Donihe — A nightmare comedy about destiny, faith, and sex toys. Also featuring Donihe's most lurid and infamous short stories: *Milky Agitation, Two-Way Santa, The Helen Mower, Living Room Zombies,* and *Revenge of the Living Masturbation Rag.* **108 pages $8**

BB-127 "Metamorphosis Blues" Bruce Taylor — Enter a land of love beasts, intergalactic cowboys, and rock 'n roll. A land where Sears Catalogs are doorways to insanity and men keep mysterious black boxes. Welcome to the monstrous mind of Mr. Magic Realism. **136 pages $11**

BB-128 "The Driver's Guide to Hitting Pedestrians" Andersen Prunty — A pocket guide to the twenty-three most painful things in life, written by the most well-adjusted man in the universe. **108 pages $8**

BB-129 "Island of the Super People" Kevin Shamel — Four students and their anthropology professor journey to a remote island to study its indigenous population. But this is no ordinary native culture. They're super heroes and villains with flesh costumes and outlandish abilities like self-detonation, musical eyelashes, and microwave hands. **194 pages $11**

BB-130 "Fantastic Orgy" Carlton Mellick III — Shark Sex, mutant cats, and strange sexually transmitted diseases. Featuring the stories: *Candy-coated, Ear Cat, Fantastic Orgy, City Hobgoblins,* and *Porno in August.* **136 pages $9**

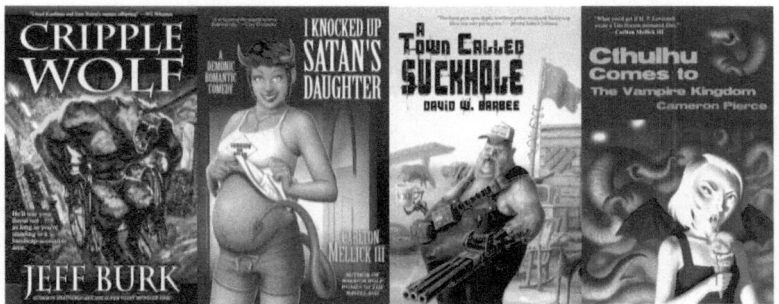

BB-131 **"Cripple Wolf" Jeff Burk** — Part man. Part wolf. 100% crippled. Also including *Punk Rock Nursing Home, Adrift with Space Badgers, Cook for Your Life, Just Another Day in the Park, Frosty and the Full Monty*, and *House of Cats*. **152 pages $10**

BB-132 **"I Knocked Up Satan's Daughter" Carlton Mellick III** — An adorable, violent, fantastical love story. A romantic comedy for the bizarro fiction reader. **152 pages $10**

BB-133 **"A Town Called Suckhole" David W. Barbee** — Far into the future, in the nuclear bowels of post-apocalyptic Dixie, there is a town. A town of derelict mobile homes, ancient junk, and mutant wildlife. A town of slack jawed rednecks who bask in the splendors of moonshine and mud boggin'. A town dedicated to the bloody and demented legacy of the Old South. A town called Suckhole. **144 pages $10**

BB-134 **"Cthulhu Comes to the Vampire Kingdom" Cameron Pierce** — What you'd get if H. P. Lovecraft wrote a Tim Burton animated film. **148 pages $11**

BB-135 **"I am Genghis Cum" Violet LeVoit** — From the savage Arctic tundra to post-partum mutations to your missing daughter's unmarked grave, join visionary madwoman Violet LeVoit in this non-stop eight-story onslaught of full-tilt Bizarro punk lit thrills. **124 pages $9**

BB-136 **"Haunt" Laura Lee Bahr** — A tripping-balls Los Angeles noir, where a mysterious dame drags you through a time-warping Bizarro hall of mirrors. **316 pages $13**

BB-137 **"Amazing Stories of the Flying Spaghetti Monster" edited by Cameron Pierce** — Like an all-spaghetti evening of Adult Swim, the Flying Spaghetti Monster will show you the many realms of His Noodly Appendage. Learn of those who worship him and the lives he touches in distant, mysterious ways. **228 pages $12**

BB-138 **"Wave of Mutilation" Douglas Lain** — A dream-pop exploration of modern architecture and the American identity, *Wave of Mutilation* is a Zen finger trap for the 21st century. **100 pages $8**